ALLISON'S PINE HARBOR SUMMER

ALLISON'S PINE HARBOR SUMMER

PINE HARBOR ROMANCE BOOK 1

J.L. JARVIS

BOOKBINDER PRESS

ALLISON'S PINE HARBOR SUMMER
Pine Harbor Romance Book 1

Published by Bookbinder Press
bookbinderpress.com

ISBN (paperback) 978-1-942767-35-0
ISBN (ebook) 978-1-942767-34-3

ONE

NOT AGAIN! Once, in college, she'd done it. Allie blamed it on poor signage, but sometimes her artsy mind wandered, and she failed to fully take in her surroundings. There she was, in the men's room doorway—again.

Allie gasped and fled down the hall toward the wedding reception. No one seemed to have seen her— not out there, anyway. But the guy at the urinal turned and saw her. Thank God she didn't know him. He would forget what she looked like, and after another glass or two of champagne, it would feel like a bad dream to her. She found an unoccupied pillar to lean on while she regained her composure.

Motion in her periphery caught her eyes. *Oh. Decker Wilmington.* She tried to look pleasant and invisible. *Please, don't.* He was heading her way. Allie casually sidled around the pillar. The nearest exit was about twenty feet away. She could make it. She ambled, taking care not to draw any attention. *Fifteen feet.* She glanced out of the corner of her left eye then the right. No Decker. She reached ten feet. *Almost there.* Then it was five more feet to the lobby. She could almost taste victory.

Once through the doorway, she took a sharp turn and pasted her back to the wall. After a few furtive glances, she spied an ideal place to hide. Across the lobby was a fireplace where, despite it being the end of June, gas flames gently licked ceramic logs. It seemed odd at first, but with good air-conditioning, who didn't love a good fire? But what really interested Allie were the two high-backed chairs facing it, perfect for hiding. One more glance at the doorway, and Decker wasn't in sight. *Good.* She proceeded slowly at first then gave up and speed-walked to the fireplace. Sighing, she sank into a chair.

Perfect. All Allie needed was a few minutes alone to calm down and pull herself together. *Decker Wilmington.* She shook her head. *Decker.* He was that kid who, from day one of kindergarten, reigned as the most annoying student in the class. He had been helicopter-parented into giving the appearance of being precocious when in truth, he'd developed too much self-esteem. From that early age, he had a way of trying to be pleasant while inadvertently landing an insult—so charming. If she hadn't known him so long, she might have thought he was deliberately condescending, but years of observation convinced her that wasn't the case. It was Decker's gift.

Decker Wilmington was wealthy in an old-money way, and he was sheltered. He seemed mystifyingly unaware of how different his life was from hers. Allie would never forget the bewildered look on his face when she told him that, no, she did not have an indoor pool, nor did she have an outdoor pool. She had an inflatable wading pool in the garage, but she chose not to share that. As they made their way through elementary school, and his understanding of the ways of the world broadened, he developed a charitable civility toward people like Allie—lowly regular people. In fact, he paid particular attention to Allie in a way that might have seemed almost kind if it hadn't been so patronizing. But small towns were like families. You got to know people well—really well. And you had to accept them because you would see them again and again, for the rest of your life or theirs.

But it was their time together in high school that cemented Allie's dislike for Decker.

DECKER HAD ASKED Allie out on a date. Why she said yes would have been anyone's guess. Perhaps it was compassion, the sort one would show to stray pets, or maybe she just wanted to go out where they didn't serve food on paper. She wasn't proud of that, but she wasn't one to lie, even to herself. The date would give her a chance to see how the other half lived. She rationalized it by viewing it as a way to repay him for carrying most of the load as her lab partner in bio. She couldn't help it if she wasn't a science-y person. She blamed genetics, which brought it full circle. It was science's fault.

Regardless of the reason, Allie went out with Decker. That would go down as one of her tragic mistakes. Looking back, she pinpointed some signs of his unrealistic expectations but dismissed them as Decker just being Decker. The dinner hadn't gone badly. Allie managed to fill most of the awkward silence with talk of school and upcoming events, but midway through the entrée, she ran out of topics and paused. Just as she thought to bring up the next week's history test, he interrupted her.

"Allie, I've wanted to talk to you."

"And here we are. Talking." Allie was a little taken aback by how chirpy she sounded. She was using her phone-call-with-strangers voice, a little higher in pitch with an upward inflection at the end of each sentence.

Decker was unfazed by it. In fact, he looked captivated. It was beginning to make her feel uncomfortable.

With a clink, he set his fork on his plate and leaned forward. "I don't know why. I can't figure it out, but I like you."

He gave her no time to absorb that bit of news before plowing on to the next. "I've tried not to. We are so not suited for each other, but I can't help myself. Allie, you've got to have seen it. I mean, how could you not? There it is. I like you."

"I like you, too, in a lab-partner-I've-known-since-kindergarten sort of way—like brother and sister." She smiled cordially, but it faded as she reflected. "Not *Game of Thrones* brother and sister but, you know, normal." Her eyes flitted downward.

Allie's heart pounded and not in a good way. She was too young for atrial fibrillation. All she could think of was how she would get home once she bolted and ran out the door. She could call home, but then she would have to explain everything and didn't want to do that. *Who do I know with a car?*

Oblivious to the torture he was inflicting upon her, Decker continued, "We can make this work. It's not going to be easy, but I'll help you."

Help me? With what? "Decker, I think you're getting a little ahead of yourself."

He smiled. "Oh, I know. There's a lot to overcome. We don't have to tell them where you live right away."

Tell whom? She might not have been as refined as he was, but she knew flinging the bread basket over the table at him would never be sanctioned by Emily Post.

Decker leaned back and lifted his chin. "It's my parents. They're going to wonder why they haven't come across your parents at the country club or a fundraiser." His face brightened. "We could tell them they're abroad but left you behind to finish high school."

"Decker, stop." She was surprised by how remarkably calm her voice sounded, considering how her true feelings were working their way from bewildered to indignant. "We're not... it's not..." She couldn't form words. All she could do was grimace and shake her head.

He smiled gently and nodded. "I know. I hate lying, too, but you don't know my parents. They will wonder. Things like that matter to them. My mother has never gotten over the—" He lowered his voice when he said, "Well, I'm not supposed to talk about it, but my father had some legal issues a while back. It cost them dearly and kept them from sending me to prep school. My mother is desperately hoping that I'll marry up and bring us all back to our former stature. A rising tide lifts all boats."

Well, this boat's not sailing today. Allie struggled to find the right words. "Decker, I'm flattered, but I don't feel that way. I guess I shouldn't have agreed to go out. It's my fault, except—it's only a date—a first date! If you think about it, we barely know each other."

"We've known each other since kindergarten. We were lab partners!"

"Yeah, but outside of the science lab..." Her eyebrows drew together, but Allie forged onward. "We've grown apart since kindergarten, and I just don't think biology is enough of a foundation." *That didn't come out right. Keep talking.* "Anyway, I'm sorry. I'll get a ride home." She set her napkin down and walked away.

He called after her bitterly, "The napkin goes on the left."

She just kept walking.

From a ladies' room stall, she made a phone call and waited until her friend Kimberly texted that she was in the parking lot. Then she made a mad dash. It was a shame how few restaurant bathrooms had windows.

FOURTEEN YEARS LATER, she was still hiding from Decker. She sank into the high-backed Bristol chair and muttered, "Ugh. I hate men."

"Sorry." The chair beside hers swiveled around to reveal that she wasn't alone, after all.

What might have been a pleasant laugh between strangers was destroyed by an uncomfortable truth. Their eyes met and locked long enough for the men's room incident to replay in her head—and apparently his, because his mouth quirked in the corner. "So, we meet again."

Allie's face wrinkled with humiliation. *Why can't I just disappear—vanish without a trace?* But no, there she was, looking at him, her men's room man. Well, he wasn't hers. He was just a guy sitting in front of a girl who had walked in on him peeing.

"I'm sorry," she said feebly. She could barely make eye contact except for the way he held her gaze with the Herculean power of his rugged good looks. It was almost as if he were doing it deliberately just to watch her squirm. He could have saved himself the effort. She couldn't have felt worse—until he spoke.

"I guess it is pretty sexist—the whole skirt and pants signage on doors. Women sometimes wear pants. I can see your confusion."

Allie's eyes narrowed, but she forced a weak smile. "Yeah, I, uh, obviously wasn't thinking." She looked down at her current attire. "Yup. Today was a skirt day." *A skirt day and a bad day.*

His smile faded as he studied her. "Be right back. Don't go anywhere." He bounded up and disappeared.

Allie muttered, "Why would I? That restroom excursion didn't work out so well. God knows what I'd do next, given the chance."

In her defense, she'd spent every weekend in June at a wedding. Now, at the last of the year's weddings, she was ready to celebrate spending the rest of the summer not watching pairs of googly-eyed couples in love. Having suffered through the longest wedding ceremony to date, she'd arrived at the reception and helped herself to two champagnes, one medicinal and the other celebratory. Evidently, they'd gone to her head.

Her new fireplace buddy reappeared with a bottle of champagne and two glasses. *Well, why not?*

"What's this?"

"Champagne."

She leveled a wry look at him. "I know it's champagne. I just wasn't expecting it." Through her lingering embarrassment, which would take some time to get over, she realized he had just made a gesture of kindness. *How nice. Or he needs a drink.*

As if reading her mind, he explained, "You looked like you could use a drink, and I knew I could."

Hmm. Confidence, charm, and a good judge of character. She wanted to smirk, but his expression was so sincere that she regretted the snarky tone she'd just tossed his way. It was too little too late, but she thanked him.

He shrugged it off and handed a glass to her. "Theo Silva."

She smiled and took the glass he offered. "Allison Pidgeon. But most people call me Allie."

He lifted his glass in a toast. "Here's to opening doors."

Allie frowned. *Not the men's room door again.* He just couldn't let that go. But when she lifted her eyes to meet his, she couldn't help but smile and stare. He looked good. But who didn't look good all dressed up for a wedding? He was also acutely attentive, which was not all that common around those parts, at least not in her experience or to that degree.

He looked at his glass then at her, as if to say, *Stop staring and drink.* So Allie did.

While he refilled her glass, he asked, "Friend of the bride or groom?"

"Bride. And you?"

"Neither, really."

"Oh. Wedding crasher?"

"Not quite." He smiled and leaned back, crossing an ankle over the opposite knee. "Technically, I'm a friend of the groom. Never met him, mind you, but my date went to school with him."

Date? Allie's hopes deflated. Until that moment, she hadn't even realized she had hopes to deflate, but she felt let down. Of course he was there with a date. Men that attractive didn't just roam the earth unaccompanied by women, especially at weddings. Not that he was perfume-ad handsome—he was more of a sporting-goods-catalog type of good-looking guy, the kind of man with buff buddies who slugged one another in the shoulder for fun. Guys like Theo tore their ACLs and broke their noses in athletic pursuits, rendering them forever unsuitable for news anchor careers. Theo would be her go-to guy if she ever found herself stranded in subzero Alaska. Or, closer to home, he would look great on a coastal Maine schooner. Clad in a cable-knit sweater, thick, wavy brown hair gently stirred by a slow-motion sea breeze, he would lift his square jaw and boldly defy the bracing salt air. A hint of color would be in his stubbly cheeks as he stood with one boot casually poised on the boat bench.

A quizzical look filled his deep-set brown eyes. "Nice wedding. They looked happy."

Allie nodded. "Forty percent of marriages end in divorce."

He leaned closer and gazed until one of them

ought to have blinked. Allie couldn't take the heat, so she turned toward the fire. It felt safer somehow.

Her mind cleared enough to think of something to say. It wasn't something clever, but it was something. "It's my fourth—and last—wedding this summer."

His eyes sparkled. "Four weddings and a urinal."

Allie's face grew hot as she forced a smile. "Thank you. I'd almost forgotten."

His lips spread to a smile as well. "Oh, I couldn't let you do that."

She winced. "Oh, yes, you could." She glanced back toward the reception.

"I'm sorry. I promise I'll stop."

Allie glared at him, full of mistrust, but it drifted away like mist when she saw the soft look in his eyes. With just that one look, he had melted her brain. *More to follow.*

Theo also seemed to have a knack for reading people well, or at least he had her figured out. He leaned back, relaxed and with an air of assurance, as if he knew she wasn't going anywhere. She wasn't but not necessarily because of him. If she thought hard enough, she could come up with a reason.

There was still some champagne in the bottle. He leaned forward and poured it into her glass. "So... four weddings and none of them yours?"

"No."

She might have answered too quickly, judging from his sudden broad smile. She reflexively smiled back at him.

He waited for her to elaborate, which caught her off guard. He almost looked like he cared what she thought. It wasn't every day a man looked and listened —really listened to her. *Not every day? Who am I kidding?* Once a month was about par, although that month was nearing an end, and she hadn't felt that level of interest—which was not a good sign, since she had a boyfriend of sorts. In truth, they were more like friends who did things together. They were placeholders in each other's lives.

And that reminded her that Justin was at the reception somewhere. She glanced about. Then her mind wandered back to Theo and his question. "No, no weddings for me." She chuckled. "That sounded a little bit sad, didn't it? I didn't mean it that way. It's just... marriage should be something you ache for. And I don't."

He looked intrigued, as if she were a fascinating woman or a science specimen. Either way, it was a magnificent look, so much so that she began to talk without knowing what might come out. "I mean, you should feel so strongly for a person that you can't seem to get close enough."

"And there's no one like that for you?"

Allie balked. "No!"

Her enthusiastic response made him chuckle.

She began talking again to fill the silence. "Life is simpler single, don't you think?" Judging by the glint in his eyes, Allie sensed she had sparked a retort, but he didn't voice it. She guessed why. "Oh! Unless you're married, in which case that would be perfect."

Yeah, just perfect. Calm down, girl. You are here with your sort-of boyfriend, whom you seem to have lost. Where is Justin, anyway? She had no idea what she was doing there, chatting it up with a stranger she'd only just met—in the men's room, no less. It was probably time to wrap up the conversation. It had gone way past small talk, and he seemed too good to be true. Five more minutes, and she would be deeply in love. *You might be overreacting a little.*

"I completely agree." He gazed frankly at her.

She'd grown so lost in her thoughts that it took her a moment to retrace their conversation.

Theo leaned forward, elbows on his knees, and stared at the fire. "People put too much emphasis on social conventions and not enough on what's important and real."

Something real happened in Allie's heart. It took flight then did a double twisting, double somersault dismount and stuck the landing.

Theo continued to stare at the fire, lost in thought.

Allie wanted to ask him what he was thinking about, but he looked so intense that she felt she would be intruding.

He leaned back in his chair and turned to her with a smile. "Damn weddings. They make people think and do things—things they should not do—like dance."

He lifted his chin as he glanced toward the door to the reception hall. No explanation was needed. Otherwise sensible adults were lined up and doing the bunny hop. Theo watched with twinkling eyes.

Allie's lanky, sandy-haired date bounded toward her. "There you are!"

"Justin! Hi. This is Theo. Theo, Justin." Her hand gesture hung in the air, as if she were a game show model wondering if she'd left the oven preheating.

Saying a hasty hello, Justin pulled Allie out of the chair by the wrists. "Hurry up."

"Why?" She cast a confused goodbye look at Theo before Justin dragged her into the reception.

As much as she could while being dragged back to the festivities, Allie studied Justin. That was weird, even for him. He'd been acting strangely for the past several days. Allie sighed with relief as they bypassed the end of the conga line—not that there was anything wrong with a good, vigorous hop around a large room like a small animal in an elegant dress. It just wasn't her thing. They stopped at the edge of the dance floor.

"Wait here. I'll be back in a minute."

Allie waited, feeling confused, awkward, and a little bit tired. The wedding was winding down. The bride and groom would be leaving, then so would she. She could complain of exhaustion, send Justin home, and curl up with a book. Allie glanced about. Yes, she was standing alone on the dance floor, no doubt looking foolish. She caught a glimpse of Theo walking into the room with a woman in a lavender dress.

"Excuse me. If I could have your attention..."

Allie's head snapped toward the sound of Justin's voice. *What is he doing with a mic? Is he drunk?* No, she hadn't seen him drink more than one beer or maybe two.

He stepped onto the dance floor, mic still in hand. A moment of panic seized her. *Justin, do not sing, whatever you do.*

He didn't. "I've got something to say. Here we all are. So many friends. So it seemed like the perfect time to share something that's been on my mind."

Your mind? Do you mean the one that you've lost? All the speeches are over. Put down the mic.

Allie froze as Justin walked toward her. His amplified voice filled the room. "Allison Pidgeon?"

People stared. She didn't have to look to confirm it, but she did.

Justin took her hand and tugged her toward the

center of the dance floor, but she dug in her heels, and he gave up halfway.

She murmured, "Justin, what are you doing?"

He released his grip on her hand, much to Allie's relief. Then he dropped to one knee.

Allie panicked. "Justin, get up. Please." She grabbed his shoulders and tried to pull him back up to his feet. For a lean guy, he was heavy. She had to leave him down there on his knee.

"Allison, we've known each other for years. And we've been dating for two."

Dating? We do stuff together. She tried, but she couldn't get the words out. She must have looked shocked, but Justin continued.

"And I hope we'll be together forever."

She started to tell him he'd misunderstood, but her ears began ringing. She couldn't think clearly. She barely heard him declare that he loved her and wanted to spend his life with her because inside her head, the word "no" echoed over and over. Then it stopped when he pulled out a ring.

"Will you marry me?"

Murmurs of delight spread through the room.

She spoke softly, hoping no one would hear. "We've never talked about marriage."

"I wanted to surprise you."

Oh, you have.

His eyes darted about then met hers. "Allie. Will you?" He waited then whispered, "Say something."

If she said yes, she would be lying. Then she would have to tell the truth sometime.

"I can't. I'm sorry. I'm so sorry."

Allie said it and ran. She didn't care where to. She just needed to get away from that place and the stares. The guests cleared a path, either out of consideration or self-preservation, because she wasn't stopping. While she ran to the door, she caught glimpses of faces, as if she were on a carousel dizzily spinning around. Just as she neared the door, a lavender cloud caught her eye—Theo's date. Theo stood next to her. Their eyes met for an instant as Allie rushed past him.

She wondered if she was destined to share every humiliating moment with that guy. The worst part was his expression. That look of stunned pity seared into her brain.

TWO

ALLIE RAN past the cars in the large parking lot. She had nowhere to go, though she didn't realize that until she reached the street. Justin was her ride home, except he couldn't be, not after she'd broken his heart and shredded the pieces in front of their circle of friends, their friends' friends, their families, and people she didn't even know but who would remember her always as the woman who turned that poor guy down.

Should I have said yes? But she would have had to follow up later with a no and explain it to everyone over and over again, as would he. It would have just made it worse. *Why didn't he tell me he was thinking of marriage?*

Allie stopped. She'd walked two blocks with no thought of where she was going. She turned down a side street. If she doubled back and headed toward her house, she would have to walk past the wedding venue again.

It started to rain. *And why wouldn't it? If only there were some way to know not to get out of bed on days like this.* Allie pulled out her phone and mumbled, "I had to ask Justin to drive. But if I had driven, then he'd be the one stranded."

"Kim? It's Allie."

"Allie? What the—"

"Kim—Kimberly—stop!"

She stopped on command. *Wow, that's a first.*

Lowering her voice, Kim said, "I wasn't yelling. I was worried about you."

"Thanks, but I'm fine."

"Yeah, you looked fine a few minutes ago when you ran out the door."

"Thanks. I'm aware." Kim took a big breath, but Allie cut her off before she could begin. "This isn't a good time to talk. I just need a ride home. I'm at the corner of Highland and Oak."

"Okay. Be there in a few."

Allie leaned back against a tree to wait, despite knowing the bark would snag her faux-silk dress. Rain dripped down her forehead and cheeks. *Well, there's always a bright side. If I break down and cry, no one will know. They'll just think it's the rain.* But the mere thought of crying drew the emotions of the day to the surface. She might have let go if the sound of an approaching car hadn't drawn her attention. Kim pulled over, and Allison sank into the seat.

Kim took in a breath, but before she could get out a word, Allie said, "Not right now." Allie folded her arms and stared straight ahead.

Kimberly cast her a sharp look. "I was just going to ask if the AC was too cold."

She had an edge to her voice, but Allie couldn't blame her. Allie wasn't her usual amiable self. She had snapped at the friend who had dropped everything to come to pick her up in the rain. "I'm sorry." Allie sank farther down the seat and turned to stare through the rain dripping down the outside of the window. She was calmed by the back-and-forth thump of the windshield wipers. It was steady and predictable, unlike her life.

How could I not have seen this coming? Justin had been acting weird—not crazy-weird but just... off. More than once, she'd caught him staring at her when he must have thought she wasn't looking. Once, she stared back and smirked, but he just looked down and smiled.

Tears welled up in her eyes. *I never wanted to hurt him. If only I'd known in time to warn him.* She liked Justin a lot. She wouldn't have continued to see him for two years if she didn't. They did things together on weekends, shared work stories, and knew what the other would order from any menu in town—like good friends, because that was what they were. Sure, there were some benefits, but it wasn't what Allie would ever call love. It was more of a habit, like a comfortable sweater one kept wearing long past its prime until no one bothered to comment because it had become a part of that person. She and Justin were like eyeglasses with tape, tourists with waist packs, or teens with thick mascara—things that, while maybe not the most elegant choices, were comfortable. Everyone had little crutches that were easier to cling to than to replace or, God forbid, do without. But crutches were only ever meant to hold up a person, not serve as a foundation for a lifetime together.

Love was something you knew you were in. Justin knew it, but it had escaped Allie's notice. *How did it escape his notice that I'm not?*

Then a worse thought occurred to her. *What if this is love? What if this is all there is to it and love is simply a dependable habit?* Maybe she'd just passed on her last chance at marriage and her future self would hate that she'd turned down the only man in the world who would ever want to spend his life with her. Or maybe her future self would thank her for realizing at such a young age—okay, not all that young—that she could be not only happy but also happier without marriage. *After all, if marriage is so great, why do nearly half of all marriages end in divorce?* Because all of those people decided they would rather be alone. Allie had skipped all the torment and arrived at the better result.

But Justin had proposed. She still couldn't get her head wrapped around it. They'd never even mentioned the L word. Well, maybe he had but always in a "Bye. Love you," sort of way, not a "Bye. I want to spend the rest of my life with you because I'm unabashedly in love with you, and by the way, let's start a family. How does six children sound?" way.

Six children? Fifty-four months of my life throwing up? Four years and six months of the prime of my life? Sure, sign me up.

When did it happen? One day, Justin was drifting off in a mouth-breathing sleep while binge-watching TV, and the next, he was proposing marriage in public.

It must have been awful for him. God knew it was awful for her. If there was anyone she knew who had not been there to see it, they would hear about it soon enough. In fact, thumbs must have been flying on phone screens before she'd even made it outside. She thanked God she'd had the foresight to take the next day off to rest up from the wedding festivities. Oh, she would rest, all right—when she crawled under the covers and never came out.

THREE

ALLIE'S PHONE chimed to signal a text message. She opened her eyes long enough to squint at the blinding sun glaring at her through the window. She put a hand to her brow as if in salute to hangovers then reached for the phone. With a groan and raised eyebrows, she read the text message from Justin's mother.

By the end, Allie could practically see the woman's red face. *When you come to your senses—assuming you have any—you'll want Justin back. So I'm warning you now: it'll happen over my dead body, you hateful botch.*

Hateful botch? That's easy for you to thumb type. She set down the phone and muttered, "'When I come to my senses...'" Allie blew air through her lips. "That's optimistic." She collapsed flat on the sofa and stared at the ceiling, wondering how else she might have responded to Justin's proposal that wouldn't have caused pain of some sort. If only she'd had time to prepare a counterproposal.

She could've said yes, pretended she was happy, and accepted everyone's congratulations—in other words, lie. But Allison wasn't wired for lying. She couldn't imagine looking into her friends' and family's eyes as she lived with that lie. Then after she told them the truth, they could never trust her again. And others would wonder what kind of person said that they were deeply in love and ready to spend the rest of their life with someone then turn around a day later and take it all back. But none of that mattered, since she couldn't have done it regardless. *So what if my would-have-been mother-in-law hates my guts now?* She would be first in a long line that was no doubt forming. That was the price Allie would pay for not falling in love and not getting engaged.

On the bright side, she lived a small town where things had a way of fading into the background eventually. Not that anyone would ever let her forget it. It would come back to haunt her at unexpected moments—like every wedding until the four horsemen of the apocalypse rode in and diverted attention from her. All she needed was to keep a low profile, at home, under her quilt, until then.

Allie looked at her watch. *Wow, only ten thirty, and I've already got a viable plan!*

Her phone chimed again. She groaned. "Oh yeah? Well, you're a botch too!" She looked at her phone, but the message was from Kim.

I've got coffee and bagels.

Allie stared at her phone. If she'd wanted to talk to anyone, Kim would be on her short list. She just wasn't sure she was ready, but Kim had been there for her after she'd fled from the wedding. The least she could do was reply.

"Where are you?"

"At your door."

Oh. She might not have been in the mood for a talk, but Kim had gone to the trouble of bringing her breakfast, so she went to the door. "You're too nice, but you know you didn't have to."

Kim walked in. "I know. But I thought you could use some cheering up."

"I'm not really ready to talk about it."

"Good. I had something better in mind."

Allie peered at Kim, dreading to hear what it was.

"Beach therapy!"

To her surprise, Allie perked up at the thought. A few hours of basking in the warm sun and the sound of the waves lapping onto the shore sounded perfect. "I think I'd like that."

Kim's eyes lit up. "I was hoping you'd say that. Now go pack. We leave in ten minutes."

"Ten minutes? What, you made an appointment?" Without waiting for an answer, she threw some things into a beach bag. "I just need to change into my swimsuit."

Kim headed downstairs. "Hurry. We're burning daylight."

TWENTY MINUTES LATER, they parked in front of a convenience store. As they walked through the door, Allie glanced toward the counter, where a familiar-looking employee was ringing up a customer. *Felicity Carver?* In an instant, a Pavlovian pit-of-her-stomach sensation returned in full force. Allie nudged Kim so vigorously that Kim lost her balance, but she quickly recovered and cast a sharp look at Allie.

Allie grabbed Kim's hand and led her to the aisle with the sunscreen and asked under her breath, "Don't you remember?"

"Remember what?"

"No, who. Come on, Kim. Don't tell me you don't remember." She leaned closer. "Felicity Carver, the mean girl who tormented us during our first three years of high school. If she weren't a year older, it would've been four."

Kim dismissed it with a smirk. "That was years ago. We've all grown up. We're mature adults, Allie."

With a mock sneer, Allie said, "Speak for yourself. I, on the other hand, have the emotional maturity of a fourteen-year-old."

Ignoring her, Kim held up two tubes of sunscreen. "Smellin' Melon or Coconut Butt?"

Allie grabbed the coconut one and headed for the snack aisle. By the time they reached the counter, Allie had nearly recovered from her Felicity lunch-table flashbacks. Even so, she took great pains to avoid eye contact while unloading her cart. As Felicity rang up the dozen or so items, Allie began to relax and let go of the past—until Felicity started humming, "Here Comes the Bride." Allie stared at the credit card reader and willed it to finish its authorization.

Felicity chuckled then winced. "Oh, that's right. You're not getting married. I completely forgot."

Thanks. I haven't. And if I did, I'm sure you'd remind me.

Felicity sighed. "Poor Justin. Broke his heart and stomped all over it."

Allie got her PIN wrong and had to start over. Her fingertips punched the touchscreen.

With a quizzical look, Felicity said, "What was it my gran used to say?"

Kim said, "Have a nice day?"

Felicity leveled a cold stare at Allie. "You can't afford to be choosy."

Kim smiled. "You too."

Allie scooped up the bag, and they rushed to the car. With a sigh, Allie sank into the passenger seat. So that was how it would be from then on.

Kim studied Allie for a moment then started the car. "Let's get out of here."

While Kim backed out of the parking space, Allie shut her eyes and muttered, "Fart Face Felicity Carver."

Keeping her eyes on the road, Kim said, "You are not going to let Fart Face ruin your day. She's not worth it."

Allie stared out the window. "She's only saying what everyone's thinking."

"You don't know that."

"Oh, I think I do." Allie let out a weak, bitter laugh.

"A week from now, they'll all have forgotten and moved on."

"I pity the person who distracts them from this." Despite her moment of misery, Allie stared as they passed by the picturesque Maine harbor with its fishing boats gently bobbing in the water. Hers was a beautiful town with a close-knit population. People were there for one another in hard times, but there was also a downside. Everyone knew everyone else—every triumph and failure and too many secrets.

Allie caught herself replaying the same "if only" inner monologue. But there was no point in *if only*. It wouldn't solve anything. The rejection had happened, it was over, and Allie had to deal with it like an adult—a calm, logical, poised adult who, ten years later, still called people Fart Face.

Kim cheerfully announced, "Here we are."

The beach was practically empty. To call it a beach was a slight overstatement. It was a small patch of gravelly shoreline punctuated by rocks and a grassy cliff. Frequented only by locals who knew where to find it, it was peaceful and quiet except for the crashing of waves on the rocks.

Kimberly reached into her trunk and pulled out a beach umbrella, two chairs, and their bag of snacks, water, reading material, and sunscreen. After slinging her bag over her shoulder and grabbing the chairs, Kim led the way down the steep path, and Allie followed with the umbrella.

Allie settled into her chair, pulled out her knitting, and let the warm sun take the edge off her recurring nightmare of the previous day. She'd practically fallen asleep and dropped a stitch in the process when three teenaged girls arrived, laughing and splashing in the water. Allie watched them and longed for the halcyon days of her youth.

From high school, she'd fallen into a comfortable habit named Justin. They should have been friends— well-defined and platonic friends. But she'd deluded herself into thinking it might become more. Or maybe she was just lazy and stayed in the slow lane because she had no pressing need to go anywhere else. In an excruciating way, Justin's proposal had prodded her out of that rut, like a cow prodded back to the herd. No, it wasn't a cattle prod—it was more of a trebuchet hurling her out of a relationship that would never have ended in marriage.

The neighboring gaggle of girls returned from the water and settled on the blankets a few yards away. *What lovely, surprisingly quiet young women.* Now curious, Allie looked over to find them leaning over a phone.

One exclaimed, "Oh my god!"

"I know!" another said.

"Ouch, that was cold!"

They laughed, and the third one said, "Play it again."

The first one caught Allie staring and returned her attention with adolescent disdain. But then the girl's expression relaxed, and her eyes opened wide. She looked down at the phone then back up at Allie, who was averting her eyes when she heard someone say, "Frigid fiancée." Intense whispering followed, accompanied by hums of agreement. "It is! It's her! It's the frigid fiancée!"

Allie turned to find Kim, ears perked, fully aware but refusing to look.

"Ignore them," she insisted, as if that were enough to make it all go away.

Kim tried to stop her as she pulled her phone out of her bag. A ten-second search of "frigid fiancée" turned up Allie's worst nightmare. There it was in striking HD video—her grand and glorious moment of humiliation digitally captured and preserved for posterity. Every moment was there, yet it almost looked like it was happening to somebody else. But the same people were there in the same room with the same decorations. And in their midst, Justin was on one knee before her.

The internet was forever. *The Frigid Fiancée? I'm not! That isn't fair!* But that didn't matter as much after she noticed how many people had viewed it. She forgot about not being able to breathe because her stomach was sinking, and she feared she might lose her last meal. *Is there anyone left who hasn't seen the worst moment of my life?*

She lifted her eyes.

Kim said softly, "Don't. It's just... stupid." She

gasped. "Not you! I mean... it's stupid the way people find entertainment in other people's misery. Not that you're miserable or... crap. I'm making it worse."

Allie shook her head. "It's okay." Then her eyes drifted down to the view count. Her face blanched as she looked up at Kim. "Have you seen the views?"

Kim reluctantly nodded.

"I've gone viral."

Kim met her distressed gaze with sympathy but without surprise.

"You knew?"

Kim opened her mouth to explain, but no words came, so she nodded. "There was no point in sharing it with you. I figured you'd find out soon enough. I just didn't think it would be this soon."

"I'm a hashtag? Hashtag frigid fiancée." Allie scowled. "I'm not even a fiancée, since I didn't accept his proposal." Allie stared at the boats in the distance. She was no longer plain old normal Allie. She had joined the ranks of the viral online sensations or, as she liked to think of them, victims. So that was her Warholian fifteen minutes of fame, not one minute of which had she ever wanted. "I've got to go." She stood and packed up her beach bag. Then she remembered that Kim was the one who had driven her here. "You stay here. Relax. I'll be fine. I'll just wait in the car."

Though she seemed a bit stunned at first, Kim rallied. "Could you give me a hand with the umbrella?"

"Sure. Sorry." Allie folded it up, shouldered her bag, and tromped up to the car.

Kim caught up with her and unlocked the trunk. When they'd packed up and plopped into their car seats, Kim's face brightened. "I know just the thing."

"Isn't that what the beach was supposed to be?"

Kim averted her narrowing eyes. "This is better. It's out of town, for one thing."

"How far out of town?"

"Far enough."

"Meaning?"

"Millerton."

"Kim, that's the next town over! People have cars. And phones!"

"It's a new restaurant—well, an old restaurant under new management." She backed out the car and drove onto the road. "My point is that no one knows it's open yet. It'll be perfect. After a lobster roll and a tasty craft beer, everything will look better!" She lifted her chin and drove on as if unaware of Allie's skeptical glare.

Everything would not look better, but the thought of eating and drinking her feelings had a certain appeal, so Allie went along with Kim's plan.

FOUR

KIM PULLED the car into the parking lot. Poised on a seaside cliff on the outskirts of town, the Silva Brothers' Brewpub had the look of an era gone by. Allie studied the weathered cedar facade through narrowed eyes. "I don't know why I let you talk me into this."

Flashing a broad smile, Kim said, "Because I'm always right, and you know it."

"Do I?" Allie pulled open the heavy oak door. "The parking lot's empty. That's good for me, but it doesn't speak well for the place."

"That's only because it's new."

Inside, the smell of chowder and freshly baked bread filled the air, drawing them in past the reclaimed-wood-plank-covered walls. Overhead, lobster traps and fishnets hung in haphazard tatters, while enlargements of old black-and-white photographs of fishermen hung on the walls. As spellbinding as the narrow old entrance was in its way, it was nothing to what awaited them straight ahead at the opposite end of the building. Tall, wavy multipaned glass windows looked past the edge of the cliff to the sea. The small dining room was practically empty, which suited Allie perfectly.

"Sit anywhere. I'll be right with you!" the bartender, who was bent over behind the bar, called.

Allie was in no hurry. She just wanted some peace, and the corner table Kim selected fit the bill nicely. Allie took a seat facing the corner where the wall met the windows and left the other chair with a view of the restaurant and its patrons for Kim. After the scene on the beach, the less anyone saw of her face, the better. She studied the menu with more interest than she had expected. It managed to marry meat-and-potatoes pub grub with seafood favorites, including a chowder whose scent called to her. She looked over her menu at Kim. "This looks—"

"I know! I'm even hungrier now. Oh, here he comes."

The bartender seemed to be the only one on duty— not that the small, empty bar needed anyone else. It had half a dozen tables at most inside and a few umbrella-topped picnic tables outside.

"Good afternoon, ladies," the man said in a warm, friendly voice.

Allie looked up into brown eyes that stared back with unsettling confidence, and she froze. *Theo? What is it about this guy that makes every nerve ending raw?* In the post-Justin phase of her life, that was not what she needed. Unable to process her responses anymore, Allie longed to find her way back to the calm and sensible person she used to be. But she couldn't do that with Theo turning up everywhere with his brown eyes and his thick hair that just barely touched his forehead over his left eyebrow. No, it was her left, his right. He had a tiny scar on his cheekbone.

Theo's eyes crinkled at the corners. "So, we meet again."

For once, Kim was silent, eagerly looking at one then the other.

Having bolts of electricity course through one's body wasn't nearly as fun as it was made out to be. Allie managed a gravelly "Theo." She cleared her throat twice. "Hello."

He turned to Kim and extended his hand. "Theo Silva."

"Pleased to meet you." Judging from Kim's broad smile, she was indeed pleased to meet him.

Still recovering her composure, Allie asked, "You work here?"

He nodded. "And I own it—half own it. My brother's the other Silva brother. There are two. Hence the halves." His eyebrows drew together.

For the first time since she'd met him, Theo seemed slightly off-balance. She was surprised by how much it pleased her to see him get a case of the stupids around her. She thought she'd cornered that market. She grinned. "Silva Brothers." Their eyes locked.

"Brewpub." He finished it for her with a bashful look that could not have been more appealing. "How are you?"

"Fine." She shrugged, which made her "fine" even worse. *Now who has the stupids?* Worse yet, he seemed to see through her and waited for her to elaborate. "Well, not fine, exactly. But you know, life is full of surprises—not all of them good—but you have to keep plodding along." *Well, Allie, aren't you just a big bowl of chicken soup for the downtrodden soul? Just stop talking, why don't you?*

To Theo's credit, he didn't try to say anything encouraging. Nothing he could have said would help— except for one thing. "Can I get you a drink? First one's on me." Soft light shone from his eyes, and it warmed her.

"Do you have any beer?"

He grinned and pointed at the name at the top of the menu. "It's a brewpub. We brew our own. The food menu is mostly for show—and to make people thirsty so they'll buy our craft beer."

His dismissive amusement didn't fool Allie one bit. His bright, intense eyes suggested a determination that his light manner belied. He was serious about his business, and Allie was serious about the aroma of fresh bread and chowder. But for starters, beer would do nicely.

Before she could decide what to order, Theo said, "I'll bring you a flight." He disappeared and returned minutes later with two flights and a basket of chips. Then he took their food order and was gone.

Intrigued by her newfound knowledge of the bar's ownership, Allie studied every wall, bar, and table with interest. It was decorated with a clean, masculine style peppered with nautical charm and a hint of industrial chic. A wood-burning stove sat in the opposite corner with two weathered chairs and a barrel between for a table. Allie's gaze drifted to Theo as he worked behind the bar.

"Who's your new friend?" Kim raised an eyebrow.

Allie rolled her eyes. "Calm down. I just met him yesterday at the wedding. Move on. There's nothing to look at here."

"Oh, I beg to differ. There's plenty to look at over there at the bar—dark eyes that look into your soul, manly shoulders and arms, and those hands!" She lifted an eyebrow. "I'll bet they can cook. And look at this place! If Mrs. Muir's Captain Gregg were a thirty-something brewmaster, he'd be this guy. What's his name again?"

Allie stared at her and said dryly, "Theo."

Kim nodded as though Allie had answered a *Jeopardy!* question correctly. "Theo!"

"Shh!" Allie cast a sideways look at the bar but saw Theo through the window to the kitchen, no doubt preparing their food.

Kim tossed a less subtle look in that direction. "Captain Theo Gregg."

"Silva." Allie turned toward the window and cringed.

Kim grinned. "You've got to love a seafaring man. And that one could splice my main brace any day, if you know what I mean."

"I don't know if decorating his business with nautical decor makes him a seafaring man. It's probably more of a location thing."

"It's close enough for me." Kim pointed at the chips. "Aren't you going to eat those?"

Allie waved her hand at them. "Have at it." She watched Kim dive in. It wasn't fair that that girl could put away food without gaining an ounce. Her mind wandered back to Theo, which was becoming a habit. She blamed it on Kim. "Anyway, he's got a girlfriend."

Why did I say that? They'd moved on. There was no need to discuss the guy's social life. They'd met at a wedding, and she and Kim were having lunch at his bar—end of story.

"How do you know that?"

"Because she was with him at the wedding."

"So? People go to weddings. They bring dates so they're not stuck at a round table with a self-absorbed couple on one side and some random traveling depilatory salesman who loves his job so much he can't stop talking about it on the other."

"Kim, it's been over a year. You've got to let that go."

Wrinkling her face, Kim protested, "He told me I had a mustache!"

Allie grimaced. "That was just some unfortunate overhead lighting."

"He offered to give me a sample." She lifted her pleading eyes to Allie's. "I don't have a mustache!"

"No, honey, you don't."

Kim looked down and pouted. "I had it waxed the next day."

Theo served their food before Kim thought to retrace the subject back to him and his date. In truth, it was the food that distracted her. The chowder was amazing, and the lobster rolls were fresh and perfectly seasoned. That along with the beer was enough to banish all thoughts of men and weddings from anyone's mind. Even Allie was beginning to envision a life after Justin's proposal.

When Theo stopped by and asked how their food was, Kim slammed her palms on the table. "Oh my gosh!" She followed up with a few heavy breaths peppered with random exclamations like, "So good! This chowder! Rolls! And this beer!"

Allie lifted her eyes to meet Theo's and smiled politely. "She means yes, everything's fine, thank you."

Looking pleased enough with both answers, Theo returned to the kitchen and left them alone.

Kim took a break from eating to take a drink of her beer. "It could never work out between us."

"Work out?"

Kim gave her a look of displeasure, as if Allie hadn't been paying attention. "Theo and me."

Before Allie could ask what she was talking about, Kim continued, "I'd be too spent after eating his cooking to think about sex. I mean, I'd have to have a cigarette after each course."

"You don't smoke."

"I know! That's how good his cooking is. But I'd be eating all day. I wouldn't get any work done. Sadly, it's not meant to be."

Allie laughed, which was a miracle after how her

day had begun. But Kim set down her fork with a sigh. "So I'll have to pass. He's all yours."

"Mine? I didn't know we were in negotiations."

Kim lifted an eyebrow and gave an emphatic nod. "Oh, we were! But sadly, I lost."

"Kim..." Allie took a moment to frame her next thought concerning Kim's elaborate fantasy life.

Before she could speak, Kim interrupted. "Let's be honest. The truth is that I didn't stand a chance. I mean, c'mon! When he looks at you, it's just... wow! Zing!"

That bit of news caught Allie off guard. She casually turned to steal a glance at the bar and saw Theo looking her way. Their eyes met, and she instantly turned back. Heat rose to her face.

"Don't look now. Oops. Too late." Kim was way too amused with herself, but her face lost its mirth. "Allie, you're blushing!"

Allie's hand flew to her cheek. "Because it's warm in here."

"Hot is more like it—and I'm not talking ambient room temperature."

Allie couldn't argue when Kim got like that. "Okay, fine. He's hot. And he's got a girlfriend. And in case you forgot, until yesterday, I had a boyfriend."

"Stop living in the past. It's today, and you don't. Oh, hi, Theo."

Allie flinched. Kim had gotten her so flustered that she hadn't even heard him approach. While he cleared their plates, Allie studied his hands. They were strong and well-formed. She could hold hands like that—or be touched by them.

"Allie?" Kim did a slight yet unsubtle eye movement toward Theo. "Would we like another round of beer?"

From the look on Kim's face, Allie guessed that she'd missed Theo's question during her hand reverie. "Oh. No, thank you."

Anyone else would have left at that point, but he lingered. It was only for a moment or two but long enough for their eyes to lock and for Allie to think he was about to say something.

Whatever momentous words he might have said were interrupted when two couples burst through the front door and headed straight for the bar. Theo smiled and gave a slight shrug. Duty called, and he went back to work.

Any void left by his unspoken words was happily filled by Kim. "He likes you."

Allie had heard those words at least a handful of times since they were in fifth grade, but Kim had always been right.

She looked frankly at Allie. "If he's got a girlfriend, his heart isn't in it. His mind is on you."

Allie didn't even try to protest. Maybe she'd felt it from the moment they met. Well, it couldn't have been the exact moment, because that would have been when she walked into the men's room. But the next moment, when they were sitting by the fireplace—that time, she'd felt something different. It wasn't the sort of fireworks display she'd always thought would accompany love at first sight. The room didn't blur and fade away like in the movies. It was more of a fog rolling in and filling her with contentment. They'd talked comfortably together with complete understanding. While she couldn't speak for Theo, it seemed as though neither of them wanted or needed to be anywhere else.

But then Justin's proposal had torn all thoughts and emotions away and left her feeling like a numb, useless blob. She was in no state to embark on any romantic journey Kim might envision for her. Her life was perplexing enough without adding Theo to the mix.

Kim paid the bill. She insisted that it was her treat. "You can pay the next time I break up with someone."

As they walked out, Allie stole one last look at Theo. He gave that gentle, kind smile of his, and once more, Allie had the sense that words had been left unspoken. But she shook off the feeling and walked out the door. The real world was out there, and she would have to face it sometime.

FIVE

THEO WATCHED Allie and her friend leave and wondered what he was doing. Yeah, she was attractive. *Attractive?* She was more than attractive. She was pretty, bright, and a little bit quirky. That shiny sable hair drove him nuts. He wanted so much to reach out and touch it. At her worst moment, as she ran past him, he wanted to whisk her away then hold her in his arms until the world disappeared. But the world was not going to disappear, nor was her baggage, which was why he had no business finding her attractive. But he did. He barely knew her, but she was on his mind more than he would ever admit. He couldn't say it was love at first sight because love at first sight was for people who cried at movies and called their pets fur babies. That wasn't Theo—far from it.

Every time he recalled the slack-jawed shock in her

face when they'd met, he smiled all over again. He pretended to wipe down the bar while he watched Allie walk by the window and head down the sidewalk. When he ran out of windows, he thought about running after her. He still had time to catch her before she drove out of his life. But he didn't.

There he was again, stalled and unable to follow his heart. Sure, he'd had relationships with women before, but he never let anyone into his heart—or his life, not that he'd planned to let Allie into his life. He had no life to let her into. And that was assuming she would want to. She had just refused a proposal. There was no way she would want a new man in her life. Even if he were to lose his mind and express interest— which he was not going to do, but still, *if*—he would wind up like What's-His-Name, left alone on one knee. The poor guy might as well have had a sign taped to his back that read Kick Me. No woman was worth being stabbed in the heart by a two-letter word.

He didn't hear his brother arrive from the kitchen until Marco stopped in his tracks and gaped at Theo. His mouth turned up at the corner.

Theo glanced at his brother with impatience. "What?"

"Enjoying the scenery?"

Theo turned and wiped down the bar with singular determination.

Marco folded his arms and leaned on the edge of the bar beside Theo. "You know, most people prefer the view facing the ocean."

Theo ignored him and sliced limes.

Moving closer, Marco said, "But I guess you're more of a parking lot guy."

Theo lifted an eyebrow but kept working.

"Or maybe it was that pretty brunette."

Theo finished the limes and picked up a lemon. "Don't you have something to do?"

Marco smiled. "What, like go ask her out?"

Theo turned with a glare. "No."

Marco leaned back. "Why not? She's cute, and she's got an available vibe."

Marco stared at the window as if deep in thought. "She's not."

Marco shook his head, seeming unconvinced. "There's available, then there's available."

"She's neither, so back off, Romeo."

"What's it to you?"

Marco took a step toward the kitchen, but Theo clamped a firm hand on his arm. "You're too young."

Grinning, Marco said, "I'm eighteen. So what if she's older? I like older women."

Theo raised an eyebrow. "And younger and every age in between."

"Guilty as charged. Excuse me. I'm just gonna run

outside for a minute." He started toward the back door that led out to the parking lot, but Theo darted toward him. Marco made it to the door before Theo caught him and held him in a full nelson.

They struggled for a few seconds before Marco burst into laughter. "I knew it! C'mon, let go. I'm not going out there. I was just busting your chops." After Theo released him, Marco grinned again. "You really like her."

Theo leveled a wry look at him. "Shut up."

Marco shook his head and shrugged. "I don't know where she came from, but I'm glad she's here."

"Except she's not. She just left, so calm down."

Marco laughed as he put on an apron and loaded a rack for the dishwasher.

Theo went back to the bar, where one of the four people at the other end of the bar flagged him down for another round, while the other three hunched over a phone in rapt attention.

"Aw, man. That was brutal," the guy at the end said.

The woman beside him sucked air through her teeth. Then they all looked at one another and burst into laughter.

As Theo served them their drinks, the second woman said, "You've got to see this."

Marco walked in just in time to hear, and he joined them. Theo's eyebrows furrowed. Videos like that were why he had sworn off social media months ago, but he saw no point in offending paying customers, so he feigned interest while Marco watched intently. The others, having already seen it, watched and waited for their reaction. A few seconds into the video, Theo didn't need to see more. He leaned close enough to verify the number of views. It was worse than he'd thought.

When it finally ended, Theo looked up as though he hadn't seen the whole thing in person just one day before. *Poor Allie. Does she know about this? How could she not?* Maybe Kim had managed to keep it from her, but it was just postponing the inevitable. At some point, Allie would see it and probably sooner rather than later.

Marco chuckled and said, "Hey, Theo. Do you have a minute?"

Theo gave him a nod and turned to the customers. "Excuse us." He followed Marco to the opposite end of the bar.

Marco wasted no time asking quietly, "Wasn't that your brunette in the video?"

"She's not *my* brunette." Still seething over the fact that someone had recorded and uploaded the video, Theo glared at Marco. He had no more patience for

Marco's ribbing. To his surprise, Marco was no longer smiling.

"But she is the woman in the video?"

Theo looked at him frankly. "Yes."

Marco's expression turned serious.

Theo tilted his head toward the end of the bar. "I was there when that video was shot. Yesterday."

Marco's eyes widened. "At the wedding?"

"Yeah. I didn't just meet her today." Marco opened his mouth and took in a breath, but Theo interrupted. "Long story. I'm not telling it now, but I saw the whole thing in person. I can't believe someone uploaded it."

"You like her."

"She doesn't deserve it."

"No, but you like her."

Theo didn't deny it. He just shook his head. "I don't think she's looking for a new man in her life—not that I was looking for anyone, either. But we met, and... there was a connection."

After a long silence, Marco said, "Sorry, man."

"Yeah." Theo made a feeble attempt to shrug it off. "Hey, could you watch the bar for a minute? I've got something to do." Without waiting for an answer, Theo went back to the office and shut the door behind him.

KIM PULLED up in front of the Gallery, Allie's tiny shop with a cozy apartment upstairs. Ten years before, in Allie's final year of art school, she'd had no job prospects in sight. Inspired by her grandmother's knitting and quilting creations, Allie had taken everything her grandmother had taught her and majored in textile design. Her grandfather attended her senior art exhibition. If the exhibition was a love letter to her hometown of Pine Harbor, it was even more of a testament to her grandmother's tutelage. Her grandmother did not live to see Allie's work on display, but her grandfather, a stalwart Mainer, slowly went from one piece to the next, taking it all in with few words. But his glistening eyes said it all.

Her grandfather had been so moved by Allie's textile art that he gave her the small storefront by the harbor. He and her grandmother had run a gift shop there for years, and he'd intended to pass the torch to Allie. She opened it first as a gallery, and little by little, she reinvested her profits to build up the inventory to create the cozy gift shop it became. Locals came by to soak up its charm, and no tourist left town without having stopped by for a Pine Harbor memory to take home, whether it was a postcard or one of Allie's wall hangings. The shop was too charming for most to resist.

Allie rummaged through her purse while Kim

parked. With her keys securely in hand, she turned to Kim. "Thank you."

"For what?" It was just like Kim to minimize the value of what she had done.

"For lunch, your company, and for distracting me from my misery."

Kim shook her head as if it were nothing, so Allie gave up and got out of the car. With a wave, she went into the shop, where eighteen-year-old Lydia sat with her chin on her hands and her elbows on the counter.

She brightened as Allie walked in. "Oh, thank god, a person! It's been so slow today!"

"Well, it is a Monday."

Lydia's large glasses accentuated her widening eyes. "No, I mean it was *slow*—all caps, sleepy emoji."

Allie tried to look sympathetic. If only a dull day were the worst of her problems.

Despite her apparent boredom, Lydia was practically bouncing with energy. "I checked in the new inventory, dusted all the shelves, cleaned the bathroom, and finished the book I was reading. All that's left is to close out the register."

Allie glanced at her watch. It was ten minutes to closing. "Go on, then."

Lydia's eyes lit up. "Really?"

Allie glanced at the empty shop. "Yes, I can manage the crowd."

Lydia bounded to the back room, her copper-colored ponytail swaying behind her, then returned with her purse. "Thanks, Allie! Oh, do you have my hours for next week?"

"I'll text them to you. Say hi to your mom."

"I will."

The shop door chimed, and Lydia was on her way home, which happened to be an apartment next door, above her friend Caroline's real estate storefront office.

Allie closed out the register, locked the door, dimmed the lights, and headed to the back of the store. There, four large windows reached up to the ceiling, while their views led out to the sea. It was a sensational backdrop for her artwork and inventory, but she'd saved a small room for herself. An unremarkable door in the corner looked worthy of no more than a broom closet, but it led to her art studio. To the right, a wood stove sat sedately with only an upholstered rocker for company. To the left, a spiral staircase led up to Allie's apartment. But the best part of the room lay almost straight ahead, where two walls of windows met at the corner, giving Allie a dramatic view of the harbor. It was in that room that Allie did most of her artwork. There, she worked every morning until the shop opened and often in the evenings as well.

That evening, though, she was in no mood for work. Her day with Kim had been a good distraction, but now she was alone with her thoughts, which were chiefly composed of an endless loop of the marriage proposal, her subsequent shock, and her sprint from the scene.

Kim had told her at lunch that everyone had assumed she and Justin would marry—everyone except Allie. She shook it off, glanced back toward the shop, and remembered. *I need to text Lydia her hours.* She reached into her purse for her phone. *What?* She dug some more then emptied the contents. *Did I leave it in Kim's car?* She thought back. The last time she'd used it was when she'd set it on the windowsill by the table. Allie knew better but went into the shop and got on the computer.

Kim answered her text immediately. *No. Checked the car. No phone here. Sorry!*

Great.

SIX

WHEN THEO TOLD his brother he had something to do, what he meant was that he needed a moment alone to wonder why he cared so much for someone he'd only just met. He ran his fingers through his hair and exhaled. That was more than enough thinking for the moment.

He turned on the computer and tried to distract himself by paying some invoices. If that didn't distract him, he was hopeless.

A minute later, he pushed back and tossed his mouse on the desk. *This is ridiculous. I've never been like this before.* It was entirely out of character. He was the sensible one who maintained control no matter what. Theo looked at the framed photo he kept on his desk, taken during earlier and happier times. He was ten, standing beside his mom while she held baby

Marco. He'd kept that photo over the years not because he was sentimental but to remind himself of his later promise to take care of Marco.

Marco burst through the door and stopped abruptly when his eyes fell to the picture. He asked quietly, "Should I lock up?"

Theo looked up, stunned, and looked at his watch. "Oh." He still felt a bit disoriented and lost in his thoughts of the past. "No, I got it. You can go on upstairs. I'll be there in a minute."

"Okay. Everything else is done. You just need to lock up."

"Thanks." He smiled, but his heart wasn't in it. The familiar nagging lost feeling had come over him again. Theo didn't know what to call it. He'd had it so long that it was just there, just something he lived with. It wasn't sorrow. He'd felt that enough and knew what it was. He didn't think he felt lonely. He just felt apart. Maybe the feeling was duty.

Theo had always been stoic or at least as long as he could remember—ever since his father had taken off for parts unknown. Theo was fifteen when his mother gathered her two little men, as she called them, into her arms. "We are going to be fine." And they knew that they would be because their mother willed it. Theo got Marco to school, made sure he did his homework, and fed him dinner while his mother went to her night job.

He was a senior when his mother got cancer, so he set aside plans for attending the local community college and instead worked two jobs. His brother would come home from school and do what he could for his mother. When she grew sicker, Theo quit his second job. Two years later, their mother was gone.

She must have known something was wrong. Before she even went to a doctor, she took out a life insurance policy, which Theo found in the bundle of papers she'd left him. He squirreled the money away in an investment account until Marco turned eighteen and graduated from high school.

Shrugging off his mood, he worked his way through the key ring until he found the right one. He was halfway to the main entrance when the door opened. He stopped and stared blankly at Allie.

"Hi." She smiled until his keys clinked together. "Oh, I'm sorry. You're closing. I'll just be a minute."

He couldn't think of anything to say. He just stood staring at her like a fool. It wasn't as if he didn't know it. Perhaps for the first time in his life, he felt simply entirely out of control.

Apparently, Allie was too kind to show that she'd noticed. With a pained expression, she said, "I left my phone here. Did you find it?"

His eyebrows drew together. "No. Hold on. Let me see if Marco found it and left it behind the bar." He'd just reached the bar when Allie said, "Never mind. Here it is." She'd gone to the table where she'd been sitting and stood with the phone in her hand. "I left it on the windowsill." She shrugged and made a funny half-embarrassed face then headed toward the door.

Theo met her halfway. "Well, good. Glad it worked out."

Her eyes shone. "I'm just glad I caught you before you locked up. I feel kind of lost without it."

Theo nodded as though he agreed, but he viewed his phone as a constant reminder of people and their expectations. "Well, good. Glad it worked out." *You said that already, genius.*

A smile teased the corners of her mouth. She'd noticed, but she refrained from full-out laughter, for which he was grateful.

She glanced down at her phone then lifted her eyes. They were open and unguarded, as if the whole world was good. "Well, I've got what I came for, so..." She glanced toward the door.

"Would you like a drink?"

It was easy to see she hadn't expected that. He wanted to kick himself. He was forcing her to say no to some poor loser. *Hasn't she had enough? Give her an out.* "Sorry. Stupid question. You're driving." *Just say yes and put me out of my misery.*

"Do you have any coffee?"

What? "Coffee?"

She grinned. "Yes." As kind as she was, he couldn't blame her for looking a little amused.

"As it so happens, I do."

Theo was almost himself again. *What is wrong with me?* It wasn't like he'd never talked to a woman. He'd even dated a few—more than a few. But he'd never felt so aware, as if time had slowed down to reveal the magic that happened between moments. It was almost overwhelming.

When things overwhelmed him, he doubled down and resisted the feeling and sometimes the cause. He lapsed into the usual Theo that charmed people—mostly women—and donned his bartender banter. When he'd brewed and poured the coffee, they went to a table by the window, where the distant lights from the harbor shimmered in broad, watery brushstrokes toward the horizon.

It was all going well until Allie asked about school. It was what people did—ask questions like "What do you do?" and "Where did you go to college?" But when Allie asked it, Theo's answer caught in his throat. "I didn't."

"Oh."

She hadn't said it with judgment. She didn't have to. Theo judged himself enough for both of them.

"I'm sorry. I didn't mean to pry. It's a bad habit. I'm

not nosy. I'm curious." She winced. "I hope they're not the same thing. I like people."

By people, he hoped she meant him. "I like people too." He meant *her*. Theo gave the same smile that always got him out of awkward moments with women, but it faded. "Life happened, and my plans for school changed."

He felt the unnerving desire to tell her everything —how he and Marco had been left with no living relatives. Theo petitioned the court and became Marco's legal guardian, which was better than plan B, to pack up and run. He'd promised his mother he would take care of Marco.

His face brightened. "Where did *you* go to school?"

The mood changed as Allie told him about how she'd majored in art.

"You're a painter?"

"Not really. I majored in textiles. Lately, I've focused on knitting and quilting."

He lifted his chin in approval. "Outdoorsy type, huh?"

Allie laughed, and Theo thought he would never tire of that sound.

She tilted her head as if studying him. "But you're outdoorsy." It wasn't a question.

"I can be. Last year, when Marco—Marco's my

brother—graduated from high school, we spent a summer hiking the Appalachian Trail."

"Oh, wow. That sounds amazing. And hard."

He shook his head and looked down. That summer was the first time he'd ever felt free, with no work and no responsibility. "At the end of this summer, we came back here and bought this place. And here we are."

Allie peered into his eyes. "I can't believe we've never met."

"I've been busy."

Allie took one last sip of her coffee. "Speaking of which, I should let you get on with your life."

Theo walked her to her car. Not even the harsh parking lot floodlight could wash out the warmth of her smile.

"Thanks for the coffee—and my phone." She was about to get into her car but turned back. "And the good conversation."

Their eyes met. *Don't feel what you're feeling. Or think it.* "You're welcome."

"Good night, Theo."

"Good night, Allie."

She closed her car door and drove off.

ALLIE PULLED out five rows of knitting she'd completely messed up, rolled the yarn back onto the ball, and put the whole thing away. She leaned back and gazed through the window at the lights on the harbor like she'd done earlier while she was talking with Theo. They looked better when she was with him.

Why? Why is it different with Theo? For two years, she'd spent time with Justin—quality time. They should have grown closer. They did, in their way, but they didn't fall in love. Correction—she didn't. How Justin managed it, she couldn't fathom. They were there for each other, so the next logical step was to be there *with* each other. She and Justin were relationship fast food. They would fall into bed to satisfy an immediate need. But people ate fast food because it was convenient, not because they didn't prefer steak.

Allie felt awful. She'd just relegated poor Justin to a fast-food burger wrapped in a thin piece of paper. He deserved better than that—a combo meal, at the least. Maybe what they were was friendship, a beverage, and an occasional side of sex. Poor Justin. He was such a good guy. Someday he would find someone who would appreciate what a great guy he was, and he'd be glad her rejection had happened. *See? Look what I've done for you, Justin.* She rolled her eyes and exhaled.

In her defense, they would still be together if he

hadn't popped the question. It wasn't as if she'd been looking for anyone else in her life. *Who else is there in this small town?* You could ask anyone, and they would say that she and Justin were a perfect match. They filled the empty calendar slots for each other. There was no drama, no complications like other couples suffered through. The four weddings she had been through that summer were perfect examples. She knew the couples well, and they had gone through near hell to arrive at the altar. The ceremony alone was daunting and, from Allie's perspective, not worth it.

Why did Justin have to go and ruin it all?

A sinking feeling crept into her gut. Justin hadn't ruined it. She had. All Justin did was love her. She couldn't blame him for that. It was practically an act of heroism that few—well, none, to be honest—had attempted. Not every man had the intestinal fortitude to endure the many facets of Allison Pidgeon. With her record, the odds that she would meet anyone else who would love her more than Justin were small. Asking to find someone she could love as much in return was just tempting fate.

More likely, she would live into her nineties alone except for a large family of cats who shared the only culinary taste she could afford. Cat food might be on the menu, but dammit, she would have her own plate.

There had been a distinct slowdown in business.

Apparently, all of her customers had sided with Justin. She'd had the temerity to let go of the only man who would have her—probably ever. In her shocked state, she hadn't realized what a defining moment it was. But with time—a full twenty-four hours—came wisdom. She'd made the mistake of her life.

Justin wasn't so bad. She could have used that in her wedding vows. Justin wasn't so bad, and they'd had some good times together. And they were invested. Two years of weekends counted for something. They finished each other's sentences and sampled each other's restaurant plates. *How could that not be love?* No wonder everyone thought they were going to marry. There was nothing to differentiate her relationship with Justin from that of any other couple who had married that summer—except love.

Maybe people made too big a deal of love. Maybe love was like money. Sure, it was great if you had it, but plenty of people lived without it and were perfectly happy. Not that Allie didn't want love. She did, or so she thought. But she wanted the love that she saw in the movies. They made it look real, and she felt it with them almost.

She wanted the real-life version of that—like that movie in which they were standing on the opposite sides of the street, then they saw one another, and somehow they knew. In some magical way, they could feel it. Her heart swelled, and his did too. Maybe. Something swelled, anyway. And a mist filled the air.

Then an eighteen-wheeler would plow through the mist and stop her from succumbing to the sheer magnetic pull of her true love's manly allure. She would step back. The truck would pass. And by then, her true love would be gone, lost to her for a good thirty minutes.

In Allie's version, she would go home to feed her nine cats, which was why Allie didn't have cats—or a love life, not even in dreams.

Real life was where she needed to focus. In her experience, the key to happiness was to adjust one's expectations. Judging by her life so far, she knew it was not going to resemble the movies. So the less she dwelled on emotions and magical mists, the happier she would be. All she needed was to get a grip on herself around Theo. On the plus side, no mist filled the air in his presence. But her heart hummed—a lot. It wasn't a musical tune. Allie hadn't quite lost her mind. She knew hearts didn't hum tunes in the key of C sharp. But just being with him made her feel as though something magical was about to happen, kind of like they must feel in the movies. Except not, because in Allie's case, nothing had happened. They'd just said goodbye and gone their separate ways. Her imaginary movie love must have been shot on nitrate film that spontaneously combusted before it got to the good part.

Allie let go of her foolish dreams, at least for the moment. She brushed and flossed, donned her onesie pajamas, and went to the safety of her fluffy quilt-covered bed.

SEVEN

People passed by the shop window, but no one came in. A few cast a quick glance Allie's way. Once, she'd convinced herself that she hadn't seen someone smirk at her, but then it happened again. By late morning, Allie felt sure her suspicions were true. People were avoiding the shop. Pine Harbor wasn't exactly Mayberry, but it was a small town, and by that point, someone would have at least waved or even popped their head inside to say hi.

She thought through the past few days' events. The proposal, or her response to it, had turned people against her. People liked Justin and her together. A cute couple, they said. They didn't say they were deeply in love. No, they were just cute. *Who wouldn't build a life upon that?*

The Pine Harbor rumor mill had outdone itself.

Curse you, social media! A pox on your pixels! To her credit, Kim had fielded much of the gossip to protect Allie. The day before, when they were at lunch, Kim had gotten a text. Allie hadn't paid much attention. They'd both been eating. Forget about Theo's good looks—that guy could cook. And as someone must have or should have said, looks faded, but cooking was forever. In retrospect, Allie should have known anything that could tear Kim away from that meal was important.

But while Kim had been intent on her phone, Allie entertained herself by surreptitiously gazing at Theo while he chatted with customers. With his tousled dark hair, deep, dark eyes, and full lips, he was easy to look at. Then there was his smile. It just spread like a cloud of dirt in a slide to home base. Home base—he could get there with her. He was definitely home run material. She could make a study of him, like those people who stood in museums in front of one painting forever. And she didn't have anything else to do at the moment. His easy manner appealed to her. He seemed to live in the moment with no expectations but always a little aloof. With no warning, he glanced at her as though he'd heard her thoughts, and he smiled. Allie smiled back and looked away, blushing but thrilled by the sense of having shared a moment that no one else was aware of. Yeah, she was losing her mind. If she lost her mind, maybe she could lose her heart too. She wasn't sure it would matter at that point.

Allie pulled herself together and turned to Kim, who quickly swiped the phone window away and slipped her phone into her purse.

"What was that?"

Kim's response was a little too cheerful, as if it was forced. "Oh, you know. Just stupid social media."

Allie had nodded, and the conversation moved on to something else. But as she reflected, she realized something Kim didn't want to share had been on that phone. She'd known Kim too long not to read her reaction. It seemed so clear now, but the day before, she was a little distracted.

Just stupid social media? She pulled out her phone to search. *But for what? What would Kim hide from me? There couldn't possibly be anything worse than the video. So why go all cloak-and-dagger on me now?* It was obviously about Allie, but she lived such a simple life, ran a shop, stayed home most nights knitting, and got proposed to at weddings. *Granted, that last one's a big one.* Whatever Kim had been hiding must be related.

Allie cringed and typed #frigidfiancée then scrolled through the results in dismay. *That's a lot of comments—a lot of harsh and cruel comments.* Kim tried to spare her, good friend that she was. She glanced at the comments then set down her phone with a grimace. Her eyes stung with tears. *Why is it always the woman's fault?* The only thing Allie had done was not fall in love. And that made her the flipping "frigid fiancée." Justin hadn't been given a name. Come to think of it, Justin's face hadn't even appeared in the video. Whoever shot it had done so from behind Justin's back, so the only face on the video was Allie's. *Lovely.*

Allie locked the shop door and went to her room in the back, which was usually her happy place. At the moment, it was her place to look out at the sea and wonder how she would ever manage to leave those four walls again. All those people who'd walked by the shop must have seen the video. Everyone in town would have seen it. It was on the internet, so the whole world could see it again and again. Even if she fled to some remote island somewhere, any random person could meet her and say, "Hey, aren't you the frigid fiancée?" Then they would laugh, elbow a friend, and point. "Hey, look! It's her! It's the frigid fiancée!" Then she would have to punch them and continue on down the road with her backpack. Thumbing rides like Bruce Banner, she would wander from town to town, picking up odd jobs and quietly trying to live a normal life, knowing that her true identity would catch up with her sooner or later—Allie Pidgeon, the Incredible Sulk.

Half an hour later, light tapping on the window brought her out of her daymare. She looked up to find Lydia's mother, Eve, outside holding a takeout bag from the deli, waving and smiling. Evelyn Parker worked at Allie's friend Caroline's real estate office next door. They'd known each other since Eve moved into the apartment over the shop. Eve was nine years older, so they were too far apart in age to have been school friends. One day, Eve stopped in the shop, and they'd barely stopped talking since. They had a standing lunch appointment on Wednesdays.

Allie unlocked the back door and let Eve in. Still smiling, Eve said, "Wow, someone was lost in thought!"

Allie wasted no time. "Do you know about the video?"

Eve's jaw dropped, and she stared in stunned silence.

"I guess everyone knows."

Eve reluctantly nodded. "Allie, some jerk thought it would be funny. Just ignore it. It's not worth it."

Allie stared blankly. *Oh, right. Just ignore it. Except that I can't!* "It had to be one of the guests, but I know practically everyone who was there. Someone I know must have done this." She glanced at the screen then gave Eve a wry look. "It was posted by Horatio Nelson."

Eve winced. "I don't know him. He must be new in town."

Allie narrowed her eyes. "The famed British admiral? No, I don't think so. I'm pretty sure it's fake." She frowned and exhaled. "Someone I know did this to me, and I'll never know who it is." She took a deep breath and let it out then saw Eve's concern. It made her want to cry more, but she didn't.

Gripping Allie's shoulders, Eve looked at her with twinkling eyes. "Go ahead. You can have a good cry if you need to. Of course, then we'd have to change the name of our Hump Day Lunch to Weepy Wednesday Lunch. And that's not nearly as catchy."

Allie almost smiled. "Don't worry. I'm not going to cry. I do all my ugly crying in private."

Eve picked up Allie's phone. "Siri, remind Allie to have a good cry on..." She put her hand over the phone and whispered to Allie, "When's good for you? Saturday? Sunday?" She shrugged then uncovered the phone. "Sunday."

A male voice said, "Okay, done."

Eve raised an eyebrow. "Your Siri's a guy?"

Allie managed a woeful attempt at a smile. "He gets me, and he's always there."

"C'mon, you'll feel better after a meal." Eve pulled Allie up from her stool and led her to the table.

"Promise?"

Eve wrinkled her face. "Well, at least you'll feel fuller."

After they sat down and started to eat, Eve laid down her fork. "You know they'll forget this by the weekend."

Allie lifted her eyes doubtfully.

"Monday at the latest."

Allie's shoulders slumped. "Everyone hates me."

"Not everyone."

"Just everyone in this town. I think they still like me a few towns over—in Canada. Mainly because they haven't met me." She took a bite of her sandwich and considered it. "I could move to Canada."

"You could, but you won't." Eve looked sympathetic, but she was also honest. "Give them time. They'll come around. It's just that everybody loves Justin."

"Then maybe *everybody* should marry him."

"You know how it is. People love an underdog, and right now, Justin's their guy. They feel sorry for him."

"Of course they do—because they weren't blindsided by a random proposal."

Eve gave Allie's hand a reassuring pat then went to the sink and refilled her glass. "You know how these things are. But take it from someone who knows. This will blow over."

"Not unless there's a Cat Five hurricane headed

our way." Allie heaved a big sigh and leaned back in her chair.

Eve's watch buzzed. "Ugh! Time's up. Gotta go." She quickly packed up her lunch bag and paused at the door. "Hang in there."

Allie nodded. Of course she would hang in there. She had no choice. As Eve headed back to her office, Allie resisted the temptation to close up shop for the day, climb the stairs to her apartment, and crawl under the covers. Instead, she took a deep breath and returned to the shop to face a long, lonely afternoon of watching customers walk by her door.

By noon the next morning, if she'd had any doubts, Allie was sure she'd been shunned or the small-town equivalent of it. It wasn't an organized shunning. There had been no town meeting or unanimous vote. But even before the technology era, small towns had developed a stunningly efficient way of dispensing with matters—and people—with every bit as much impact as the full force of the law. Word spread over back fences, and judgment was passed. Allie was going to be punished. She was grateful to live in the twenty-first century. If she'd lived in colonial times, she would be in the stocks. There was no point in protesting the unfairness of it all. She'd seen it before, just not firsthand.

Allie would not let it get her down. She proceeded to dust every shelf in the shop, checked in a box of new inventory, dusted and polished the counter, and wiped down the monitor and keyboard. Finally, she cleaned the front window glass, inside and out, then sat on her stool and sighed. *Now what?* With renewed vigor, she recounted the cash, arranged the bills so every one faced the same way. She lined up pens and paper clips to form an impressive array. With that done, she picked up a book but kept reading the first page over and over again without remembering a word she had read.

Allie slammed down the book. "That's it!" She had made a decision. She was closing the shop for the holiday weekend. It wasn't like she would lose business. And besides, she hadn't taken a day off in six months, except for the time she'd tripped on the spiral staircase, broken her toe, and gone to the doctor. It might have been the Fourth of July, but the holiday weekend would be her Allie-day weekend.

I'll do whatever I want to do. And dammit, I will be happy.

Once she'd made the decision, her spirit brightened. She began thinking of all the things she could do. The time off would be different. She was alone. Alone was a good thing, especially since she hadn't had very much quality alone time in her two years with Justin. Yes, being alone would be better than good.

Allie turned the key in the lock. She had done it. She had taken charge of her life.

EIGHT

THE LUNCH RUSH at Silva's was winding down, and the last dining room guest walked out, leaving a few customers scattered about the bar. A pretty woman in a lavender T-shirt, jeans, and a black server's apron was filling the salt and pepper shakers and set her tray on the bar. "All finished."

Theo looked up from the case of beer he'd just opened. "Thanks, Mel."

She slid onto a barstool. "I was busy there for a while. Business has really picked up."

Theo grinned. "It has." That was an understatement. They'd developed some regulars during the off-season, but with peak season in full swing, it looked like their summer earnings might carry them through the year. That meant a sense of security for the Silva brothers.

Mel leaned on her elbows and smiled. "You know, I could stay on through happy hour if you needed me."

"Thanks. We're good for today, but I'll keep that in mind."

Mel untied her apron and rolled it into a small bundle. "We're closed on July Fourth, right?"

"We'll open for lunch but close early—in plenty of time for the fireworks display. Don't worry."

"I wasn't. Actually, I thought we had such a good time at the wedding, we might give the fireworks a try." She smiled.

The offer caught Theo off guard. The wedding, as she'd presented it to him, was a one-off. Or maybe he'd just assumed that. No, she had clearly explained that she hated to go to weddings alone, seated at a large table with strangers. It would help to have a friend along with her. At the time, after he'd been trapped in the bar for days on end, the thought had some appeal. Or maybe she'd just caught him in a weak moment. In any event, he'd said yes, and they had a good time. The whole thing was very platonic, or so he thought. But that spark in her eyes didn't say friendship. He hoped he hadn't done anything to mislead her. Regardless, he needed to gently put distance between them. "Sounds like fun, but I've got plans."

Her look of pleasant surprise nearly hid her disappointment, but Mel was smart. Theo felt sure she would read between the lines. Having plans was a nice way of saying "I don't want to." She straightened her posture and brightened her eyes. "Oh, okay. No problem. I'd better get going." She flashed a smile and left for the day.

Marco appeared out of nowhere. "She likes you, you know."

Theo didn't dispute it. "I'm not what she wants."

Marco leaned back with disbelief. "That's funny. She seems to think so."

"Well, she's wrong." Theo gave his brother a wry look. "Not gonna happen."

Marco shrugged and walked through the swinging doors to the kitchen then did an about-face and walked back. With an overly dramatic slap of his forehead, he said, "It's that gallery girl, isn't it?"

"Gallery girl?"

"Yeah, the one from the little gift shop in town, the Gallery. What's her name? Allie. Yeah, that's right." He gestured toward the window table where he'd had coffee with Allie. "I saw you two huddled over there with your heads together."

There was no point in arguing with Marco. It would just make it worse. Besides, he was right. Allie interested him. The Gallery connection was news to him, though.

Marco swung onto a barstool as if it were a saddle then leaned his chin on his hands. "Ask her out."

Theo balked. "No." He didn't want to spell it out, but there was no other way to get Marco to back down. "She's the one in that video, remember?"

"Oh, right. The frigid fiancée."

"Hey!" Theo used the same scolding tone he'd used to use on Marco when he was a kid.

Marco lifted his hands. "Not my words! Whoever posted it said that."

"You don't have to repeat it."

Marco shook his head as if in defeat. "Look, man, I get it."

"No, you don't."

With only each other, they'd grown close over the years—close enough to read each other's moods. A look passed between them. "You like her, but you're not getting anywhere with her."

That annoyed Theo. "No, I wouldn't say that."

Like any eighteen-year-old who thought he could solve the world's problems, Marco got back to the point. "Then ask her out."

Theo deliberated whether to walk away without responding, but he knew Marco. It wouldn't end there, so he looked straight at him. "She's unavailable— emotionally. And I'm not looking for..."

Marco straightened up like a bird dog who'd spotted his prey. "What?" He looked almost sincere.

Theo knew not to engage, but he couldn't help himself. "You saw the video. She said no."

Folding his arms, Marco said, "To some guy. Not you."

Theo did his best to spell it out clearly. "She's just ended a serious relationship."

Marco blew air through his lips. "You don't know it was serious."

Theo was losing his patience. "He proposed. I'd call that serious."

"And she said no. I'd call that *not* serious." Marco's eyes shone with smug triumph.

"However serious it was, it was still a relationship. She's got baggage, and I'm not a bellhop."

"Theo..." Marco shook his head with such pity that Theo couldn't help but laugh.

Theo wondered why he was even bothering. "I don't want to be her rebound guy."

Marco threw his hands in the air. "Why not? That is such a sweet deal."

Theo waited. *This ought to be good.*

"You get to have all the fun with none of the commitment. It's a no-brainer, bro. No one gets hurt." Marco's grin faded. He studied him until Theo had to look away. "Oh, man. *You're* afraid *you* would get hurt!"

"No, I just don't want to get into the middle of someone else's mess."

Marco nodded mockingly. "Oh, okay. I get it. *You're* the one who's emotionally unavailable."

Theo shook his head and glanced at the door, planning his escape. "Just not interested."

"No, 'cause that would mean putting yourself out there. Which you won't. When's the last time you went out?"

"Sunday."

"Not counting the wedding. That was more of a favor."

"Been busy." That was no lie. Since he'd become Marco's guardian ten years before, he'd put his life on hold. He had enough to deal with, just trying to parent his brother without complicating things with a relationship. He exhaled. "This wasn't part of the plan."

Marco's expression softened. "So change plans. Reach out."

He would not let it go, so Theo headed for the kitchen. "She doesn't need another unwanted guy in her life."

"No, but she might need a friend. And you definitely do."

"Bye, Marco."

As Theo walked through the swinging doors, Marco called after him, "It's the twenty-first century. Boys and girls can be friends."

Theo rolled his eyes and kept walking. If he'd needed advice, he would have asked for it.

THEO SLID the computer keyboard forward, combed his fingers through his hair, and buried his face in his hands. He was acting ridiculous, like a thirteen-year-old boy, not a man pushing thirty. He rubbed his face, smoothed down his hair, and braced himself. *Allie, what is it about you?* He could sit around and wonder, or he could do something about it. *Dammit, Marco.*

He strode from his office to the bar, where Marco was chatting it up with two female patrons. "Marco, would you watch the place for a couple of hours?"

Marco held Theo's gaze for a moment. "Sure, no problem."

Ignoring the glint in Marco's eyes, Theo left.

Behind him, Marco called, "Take your time."

He could practically hear Marco mentally gloating.

As Theo hung up his apron, he caught a strong whiff of the fabric, then he held up his arm and breathed in—stale beer, ripe kitchen odors, and an even riper Theo. *Great.*

After a hot shower and a fresh change of clothes, Theo headed out the door. He didn't know exactly where the Gallery was, but the main stretch through town was no more than a ten-minute walk, so he drove into Pine Harbor and parked his pickup in the municipal lot. Within a few minutes, he spotted the Gallery. A small storefront on the edge of the main shopping area, it was white with large shop windows and a recessed entrance.

What am I going to say? He'd thought through it the whole way over. It didn't have to be Shakespeare, he kept reminding himself. *Hello. Would you like to have coffee?* That wasn't hard. He'd done as much with dozens of women before. *Why is this one different?* He took a deep breath and crossed the street.

The shop door was locked. He tried it and looked inside, thinking the door might be locked by mistake. No, no one was inside. The Gallery was definitely closed. For some reason, he tried the door again. *Because I'm thorough?* No, it was because he was pathetic—and disappointed. The mere fact that he was so disappointed drove home the extent of his interest in Allie. He'd really been hoping to see her and chat, as they had at the wedding. Conversation with her had been so light and effortless.

Oh well. Maybe some other day. Yeah, right. Why go through this again? Wasn't this torture enough?

Since he was already in town and had some time to himself, he decided to get some coffee and go sit on one of the benches scattered along the length of the pier. The summer sea breeze would cure what ailed him. Well, not really, but it would give him a moment of peace from the bar and from Marco. He loved his brother, but lately, Marco seemed to think he knew it all—more than Theo, and that was just annoying.

Theo put a lid on his coffee and headed for the pier. It was crowded with tourists, which wasn't unusual that time of year, but it was a holiday weekend, so it was even more crowded. Yet he managed to spot Allie at the end of the pier, as if he had some sort of radar for her alone. One casual conversation at a wedding, and look at him. Gulls circled and sounded as if they were laughing at him. Theo couldn't blame them. He seemed to be emotionally arrested at age eighteen, the year he took over parenting his ten-year-old brother. While other guys his age played beer pong and lived their best lives in college, Theo went to parent-teacher conferences and took Marco to soccer practice.

Though he was never a monk. He'd known plenty of women. He just hadn't had a relationship with any of them—at least not one that lasted more than a month. That was how long it took most of them to want more. He didn't have it to give. His life had enough complications. The last thing Theo needed was love. *Then what would I do? Get married and start a family?* He already had family enough, and the responsibility weighed on him. He could barely support the two of them and put money aside for his dream business, and he refused to touch a penny of the life insurance money their mother had left them. That was part of the plan. If he could keep saving, in ten years, they would have enough money to buy a small bar. But the only way to get there was by keeping life simple, just Marco and Theo. There was no room for anyone else.

And he'd done it. But now Marco was eighteen, the same age Theo had been when he'd been forced to become a full-fledged adult and parent. Marco could take care of himself. In fact, Marco would like nothing more. Getting Theo involved with a woman would take the focus off of him. Theo couldn't blame him for that.

Maybe Marco had a point. Maybe it was time to move on with his own life. He'd arrived at his goal. And there was Allie, staring out at the sea. Maybe they were both at a crossroads. Theo stood poised to approach her and talk. Despite the gulls' laughter, he headed toward the end of the pier. The breeze tossed her sable hair as she lifted her face to the sea. The wind billowed her T-shirt then flattened it against her rolled-up blue jeans. She looked free and at ease.

"Ew, look. There's Allie Pidgeon."

Theo turned slightly toward the voice and saw two young women walking behind him. Theo matched his pace to theirs.

The second one said, "She's such a Pidgeon-hole."

They both laughed.

"Poor Justin. What makes her think she's too good for him?"

"I know!" The second one leaned closer and lowered her voice when she said, "Why would you do that to someone? She could've just said yes and not embarrassed him."

"I know, right?"

They leaned even closer and spoke almost in whispers. The word "cancel" was mentioned. *Do they mean the Gallery? Are they boycotting the Gallery? Is it just these two, or are more involved?* Poor Allie. He could only imagine her life since the proposal.

He stood at a rail on the side of the pier and watched Allie perched at the end. He wanted to do something to rescue her somehow. But he had no idea what to do. He couldn't change the minds of the Pine Harbor residents any more than he could change the tide. But in time, the tide of opinion would, if not change, then be distracted by some other unfortunate neighbor or friend. It was the way of small towns. All Allie could do was just wait it out. In the meanwhile, time would pass slowly. Maybe Theo could help her with that. Or he would be one more roadblock on her way to happiness.

His gaze rested on Allie for one moment longer, but that was the moment Allie decided to turn and head back from the end of the pier. *Turn and go, Theo. Walk away now.* If he stayed, she would see him. *So what?* If she saw him, they would say their cordial hellos and move on with their days. No harm, no foul. Neither owed anything to the other. *But what if things were different?* Theo exhaled. *But they're not.*

Theo shifted his weight, ready to pivot, then stopped. *Who are you kidding? You like her. Just do it. Go talk to her. See where it goes.*

See where it goes? Where could it go? Could it— could we be something? It was such a strange thing to feel. Theo barely knew what to call it. For ten years, he had been so determined to be there for Marco and to give Marco the childhood Theo had had. He'd failed, of course. It had been an impossible goal. But at least he had managed to give his little brother a stable home —an anchor in a world that could change in an instant. He had done that not always well but the best he was able. For all his shortcomings, Theo at least knew he'd done that.

This could be Theo's time. Maybe for once he would let go and let himself care for someone. He looked at the horizon. The brilliant blue sky dipped down to meet it, and the sun scattered iridescent slivers of light across the water. There in the center was Allie. And Theo felt hope.

In that vulnerable moment, she looked at him as if she'd known all along he was there. Their eyes locked. Allie's lips parted as if she might smile, and Theo smiled back.

Her eyes darted past Theo, and in that instant, her expression changed. He turned to follow her gaze. Justin walked by him and kept walking until he reached Allie. They stood face-to-face. Her eyes darted to Theo. She almost looked lost. Then she smiled and greeted Justin.

Theo caught himself staring then turned and walked briskly away. He followed the sidewalk that skirted the water. *This worked out well. I should never have listened to Marco.*

He replayed the events on the pier in his mind. *Was there any other way it could have turned out? If I had approached her sooner instead of lurking at the edge of the pier and gawking at her like a preteen, would it have changed things? Should I have cut Justin off at the pass and staked my claim on Allie?* No, caveman moves weren't quite Theo's style. Besides, maybe she'd wanted to speak with Justin. They'd obviously planned to meet there. Theo would have been in the way. Inserting himself into the situation would have been presumptuous, strained, and ultimately humiliating. He and Allie were nothing to each other but two people who'd met at a wedding and passed a few moments together.

NINE

"Allie."

She and Justin stood face-to-face for several moments.

Someone needed to break through the silence, so Allie said, "How are you?" As soon as it was out, she regretted it. *How could he be? Why not just rub salt into the wound?*

Justin looked almost amused. "I've been better."

"Of course. Stupid question."

"No, that's okay. I know what you meant."

Allie struggled for words. Anything that came to mind would have been wrong. She missed the way things used to be. She missed their friendship. But that was gone, and there was no turning back.

"Allie, I'm sorry."

"Me too." That sounded lame, but so did everything else she thought about saying.

He looked away and swallowed. "I know I have only myself to blame for what happened."

"There's no need to assign blame."

He looked at her directly. *Does he feel it too?* Relief washed over her. It would have been inappropriate to express it. She couldn't say she forgave him. It implied he had done something wrong. But she sensed it— forgiveness and relief, or something akin to it, reflected in his eyes. It felt good to be back in that place they'd once shared. At the same time, she knew they wouldn't meet there again.

He smirked. "I misread things."

Allie's brow furrowed. She wanted to protest, if only to put him out of his misery, but he was right. That was what he had done and in a huge way. She couldn't pretend otherwise.

"I should never have put you in that position."

He was right again, but Allie knew he had done it out of love. As his friend, she wanted to be able to share his pain with him. But she couldn't. They were on unequal footing, and that wouldn't change. From now on, it would loom between them. They could never go back.

Emotion caught in her throat. "In my way, I loved you. I just couldn't—"

Justin interrupted. "I know."

Allie wanted to put her arms around him or kiss him on the cheek, neither of which would have helped.

"Goodbye, Allie. See you around." He flashed a warm smile, but the pain in his eyes told the truth. As if sensing he'd revealed too much, Justin turned and walked away.

A LITTLE PARK on a hill overlooked the harbor, so Theo headed there to finish his coffee and take a few moments of solitude to rearrange his priorities. He'd barely settled on a park bench when two women on the other side of the playground put their heads together, whispered, and eyed him suspiciously. The next instant, they called their children over to them. *Great. They think I'm a pervert!* He got up and headed for the parking lot, wondering when his life had become so absurd. Of course, he knew the answer—the day he'd met Allie. *What is it about her that makes me forget myself?* He'd perfected the art of maintaining his distance, but all that was gone. He'd met Allie and let himself care. Theo laughed. *Let myself?* He'd never had any control. It just happened. She was different, and he was all in from the start. He wanted to discover everything about her.

The best thing to do was to forget her, return to the bar, and get on with his life. The quixotic adventure was all Marco's fault.

No, it wasn't. Theo knew better. Marco might have encouraged him, but he hadn't made Theo hop into his truck and drive there on a ridiculous quest to find love.

Love? Who said anything about love? Theo took a deep breath and exhaled.

ALLIE WATCHED JUSTIN WALK AWAY. An overwhelming urge for solitude rushed over her, but that wasn't going to happen on the crowded pier. She needed to sit for a moment and gather her wits. On the nearest bench, a young mother laughed with her two preschool-aged children and wiped dripping ice cream from their wrists with a soggy napkin.

Allie's home was five minutes away, but the route felt like a gauntlet. Anyone from the community could pop into view and force her to act as if nothing were wrong. She considered her options. The sidewalk was out. At that time of day, it would be crawling with people, some of whom would be locals eager to torment her. Instead, she could skirt the parking lot and walk through an alley to the back of her store. It wasn't a foolproof plan, but it was the least populated one. And it worked. She walked the perimeter of the parking lot and made the turn to the alley. Her home was in sight.

"Allie?"

Her back stiffened. *What made me think I could sneak through the middle of town undetected?* In some ways, she supposed it was better to get the post-wedding greetings done so she could move on with her life. But she really did not feel ready. So she pasted on a smile and turned. Then she took in a sharp breath. "Theo." She marveled at how he made her heart leap. Well, he was pretty hot. But she barely knew him—or his girlfriend, she reminded herself. She smiled, which she wasn't doing very much lately.

He came to a stop a few feet away. Their eyes locked. The only indications that time hadn't stopped were the squawking gulls overhead—and his voice. "It's good to see you."

"You too." Allie meant it. Theo was separate from the drama that plagued her life. With him, she felt lighter and better able to breathe.

"How's the brewpub?" *Duh. How would it be? Running a fever? Exhausted from all the hard work? It's a bar. People drink. People eat. It just sits there.*

He flashed a smile that lit his eyes. "I left Marco in charge." He added as an afterthought, "My brother. Did you meet him when you were there?"

Allie slowly shook her head. "I don't think so."

"Oh, you'd remember. Marco has a way of making his presence known to pretty women."

Did he just call me pretty?

"When I left him, he was chatting it up with some ladies at the bar." He lifted his eyebrows and smirked.

Allie laughed and thought about what he'd said. *Pretty?* He must have meant Kim with her long sun-bleached hair and light, fun-loving manner. Most others paled in comparison.

His smile faded as he looked away and looked back. "Would you like to get a coffee?"

She tried not to look thrilled that he'd asked. *It's only a coffee, and he has a girlfriend. Don't be silly.* The question had caught her entirely off guard, as if she'd never been asked out for coffee. Friends did that, and that was all he was trying to be—if that. Maybe they were meant to be friendly acquaintances. Her eyes darted away and caught sight of a to-go coffee cup in his hand. If she hadn't stared at it, he might not have noticed. But he did. He looked down at his hand and winced.

For some reason, his every expression enthralled her. Maybe she'd been with Justin so long that she'd forgotten that feeling. No, it was new. She'd never felt it before.

Theo glanced toward a trash can a few yards away and lobbed the coffee into it. He looked back at Allie with a bashful grin. "Busted. I don't care about coffee." He shrugged and confessed, "I like talking to you."

What can a girl say to that? "I love coffee." She also loved how relieved he looked.

"Shall we?" He tilted his head toward the street, where a coffee shop stood just around the corner.

Her high spirits sank as she envisioned the crowded cafe. Going there could mean seeing people she knew—maybe even Justin. After all, she'd just left him a few minutes before. To walk in with Theo would only add grist to the rumor mill. It would be better to decline Theo's offer. Then a feeling of anger set in. She had every right to have coffee with Theo. Mean-spirited people were not going to control her life.

Theo waited for Allie's response with a doubtful expression. "Sorry. Is this a bad time? I didn't mean to presume."

She realized she was frowning and forced it away. "No! I'd love coffee." *But not at the coffee shop.* The last thing she wanted to do was drag him into her drama. The mere mention of anything Justin-related would ruin the moment, which so far was perfect. "The coffee shop can get pretty busy. My shop's just over there. I've got coffee. And there's no line."

"Sounds good."

THE BACK DOOR of the shop led into Allie's private back room. Theo stopped and took in the view from the window. "Wow, this view is breathtaking."

"I know. I lucked out, didn't I?" On the opposite side of the room stood a sink and a small counter with a one-cup coffee maker. She got to work on the coffee while Theo turned from the view and took in the room. He glanced about approvingly then went to the inside door. "Does this lead to your shop?"

"It does. Sometime, I'll take you on a tour." She smiled and hoped he would drop it.

He didn't. "Would you mind if I took a look?"

She did mind, but she couldn't tell him that. "Sure. Help yourself." It would be just her luck that someone would walk by and see them together. The shop windows were like a fishbowl where everyone could find out the latest in Allie's remarkable life—as if they hadn't remarked enough about it already. Part of her wanted to believe she was overreacting, making too much of whatever was happening with Theo. But she wanted to protect it. In an instant, one person could ruin it before it ever started. *Started?* She was delusional. People invoked that word as if it was a bad thing. So far, she loved the delusion.

He went straight to one of her paintings of a weathered boat half consumed by the sand. "Who's the artist?" He looked closer. "Allison Pidgeon?" He turned toward her.

Allison lifted her shoulders and made a face. She was going for graciously modest but was sure her spread lips and clenched teeth looked more goofy than gracious. He leaned closer and studied the painting.

"Don't look too close, or you might see the numbers."

He laughed, much to Allie's relief. Not everyone got her brand of humor.

She glanced toward the shop window and spied a pair of women she knew on their way down the sidewalk toward the Gallery. If she hurried, she and Theo might avoid being seen. She spoke a little too quickly, "So, this is the shop. Hey, it's such a nice day. Let's go out back to the patio for our coffee." To her relief, he agreed. She got him through the door just in time to see the two women pass by as she whisked the door closed.

The tiny patio was carved out of her parking area, leaving space for one car beside it. Deck rails and a three-foot-high hedge enclosed the space, leaving room for two chairs and a view of the harbor. As they sat, Allie said, "I like sitting out here. It helps clear my head—not that it's all that crowded in there."

Theo didn't laugh that time but looked into her

eyes with a curious expression. "What thoughts need to be cleared?"

"Oh, you know, things... people... the usual."

She could see that her answer hadn't satisfied him, but he didn't press for more. After a moment of scrutiny, he set down his coffee, leaned back, and looked out at the harbor, stretching his legs out before him. He had strong thighs and muscular calves like a runner or maybe a cyclist. He broke into her reverie and asked how long she'd lived in Pine Harbor. Her whole life, she told him. They talked about the town and the things people did to pass the time. Then they moved on to share their life stories—the abridged versions. Over the next hour, they managed to touch on a surprising number of topics—everything but the wedding, which suited Allie just fine. At one point, she nearly asked about his girlfriend, but that would have opened the door to the wedding. She wanted so badly to ask but lost courage. Or maybe she didn't want to know the truth. If he and his lavender lady were madly in love—or worse, engaged—she preferred not to know.

The Methodist church in town seemed to choose that moment to interrupt Allie's bliss by chiming the hour. Theo looked at his watch. "Sorry, I've taken over your afternoon. I'd better let you get on with your day."

Allie shook her head. "It's fine. I took today off. The Gallery's closed." Fearing she might sound a bit desperate, she added, "But there are always things to do... Gallery things."

"Marco will be wondering where I am. Can I cut through this alley?"

Allie stood with him. "Sure. It's a common area for the shop owners, so as a shop owner, I give you permission." She gave him a slow, regal nod.

He looked into her eyes. "I enjoyed this."

"Me too." *And I'm enjoying this moment. So don't stop now.*

Electricity arced between them. It must have been how the Bride of Frankenstein felt as sparks sprayed from the lab equipment. *"She's alive! Alive!"* Or maybe it was just an arc fault. She couldn't trust electricity or her feelings.

Theo looked down at her lips, and she thought he might kiss her. She tried to write it off as wishful thinking, but something was there. He had to feel it too. He smiled gently, said goodbye, and walked back to the parking lot where they'd met. She resisted the urge to run after him and fling herself onto his back while hooking her legs about him. *Would that look too desperate?* But she couldn't just stand there in the doorway and stare as he walked down the alley. Well, she could, but if he turned around, the drooling might be off-putting. Looking away took some real willpower because the view was spectacular. Instead, she closed the door and rushed to the window to peek through the blinds. *Because that's not pathetic. Remember. You're friendly acquaintances.*

She turned and headed upstairs but stopped halfway up. *Or maybe you're friends. But that's it. The butt—buck—stops there.* She took a few more steps then stopped again. *But it is a nice butt.* She glanced down toward the door. *Get a grip—not of his butt. He's a guy who's your friend. He's a very attractive guy who's your very attractive friend. You've had guy friends before.* She wrinkled her face. *That's how it started with Justin, and see where that got you! But this is nothing like that.* She shook her head and finished climbing the steps and arrived at her apartment. *I would love some hot chocolate. And Theo.*

She busied herself making hot cocoa then sank into her favorite chair and turned on the TV. As she scanned the directory, her mind wandered. She set down the remote. Cocoa in hand, she leaned back and stared out the window at the blurred reflections of lights on the water. She and Theo had definitely shared a moment before parting. No one could dissuade her of that. But that was all it was, one moment. And she might have misread it. She was wasting time obsessing over one second in time, a tiny blip in the grand scheme of things.

Maybe that lingering gaze was because at some

point, she'd rubbed her eyes, smudging her makeup. He might have been pondering whether it was makeup or if she'd walked into a door. Plenty of things caused people to stare. *Wait a minute. Did I smudge my makeup?* She set down her mug and sprang out of her chair for a look in the mirror—no smudge and no black eye. Her hair looked a little frizzy, though.

She thought back to Theo's deep gaze. *What was that?* Allie rolled her eyes and blew air through her lips. He was probably trying to remember where he had parked. *Yup. That's it. That's all it was. He's just my friend Theo—not boyfriend, just Theo, my friend.*

TEN

Lydia heard voices outside and glanced up, but the people kept walking. She put down her crocheting and leaned her chin on her hands. It had been another slow morning at the Gallery. The occasional tourist wandered in, but no one from town had stepped foot in the shop since the wedding. It didn't take a genius to figure out something was up. She pulled out her phone. Two minutes on social media and a few texts confirmed her suspicions. A small group of friends loyal to Justin had taken it upon themselves to put things right, by which they meant that they were determined to exact revenge on Justin's behalf.

The door opened, but it was only Eve stopping by to see how things were going.

"Hi, Mom." Lydia barely glanced up from her phone.

Eve joined them at the counter. "Do you think being on the phone looks professional?"

Lydia gave her mother a wry look and swept her upturned hand to indicate the empty shop. "Mom." She paused to sigh. "No one's here. No one's been here. Know why? Here's a sample."

Eve leaned over Lydia's phone then took it and scrolled down. When she'd read enough, she looked up to meet Lydia's knowing expression. "I can't believe this." She glanced back at the phone and pointed. "Although that one? Not a shocker."

"Oh, I know. She's so mean. But poor Allie."

Allie whisked into the shop. "Poor Allie what?"

Eve and Lydia glanced at each other with round eyes then turned to Allie with blank faces.

Recovering first, Eve said, "Sorry. It's nothing."

Lydia chimed in to the rescue. "We were just... Something reminded me of the wedding and what Justin did to you and—sorry, we didn't know you were there."

"I come here often." Allie smiled, but it faded. Her eyebrows drew together as she glanced at the phone in Eve's hand.

Eve looked at her bare wrist. "Oh, look at the time. I'm due back in the office." She gave Lydia the phone. "Bye, you two. See you later!"

Really, Mom? Smooth.

Allie asked, "What's on the phone? Never mind. I don't want to know."

It pained Lydia to see the look on Allie's face. "I take it you haven't been on social media lately."

"No, the video was enough, so I put it away. I check my phone for messages and voice mail, but that's it."

"I'd stick with that plan," Lydia said sympathetically.

Allie nodded. "It's pretty obvious someone has spread the word to boycott the shop, if that's what you're talking about. I mean, look at this place. Worse yet, look at the register. It's the middle of summer, the height of the season."

"I'm sorry, Allie. They're all ugly and mean."

Allie pouted in agreement. "And their mothers dress them all funny."

They burst into laughter, but it didn't last long.

"It'll pass. Right?"

Lydia nodded reassuringly and almost convincingly. She couldn't help but wonder. The boycott would end but maybe not soon enough. She didn't know much about Allie's finances, but she knew how her mother struggled to pay all the bills. At least her mother could count on a regular paycheck. For Allie, no customers in the shop meant no income at all.

Allie leaned closer and peered at Lydia. "Hey, wipe that worried look off your face, missy. I'm fine."

Lydia thought of the new laptop she'd been saving for. That new college computer was sprouting wings. "If you need to cut some of my hours, I'll understand."

For the first time, Lydia saw a crack in Allie's confidence as tears moistened her eyes. "That is not going to happen. But you are so sweet to suggest it." Allie smiled then turned away to conceal her emotions. She suddenly brightened. "You know, I've been thinking of shifting a few things around in here. What would you think about swapping these needlepoint kits with that new yarn? It looks lost in that corner, you know?"

Lydia looked and nodded. "Yeah, I can see it."

Allie grinned. "Let's go nuts and shake things up around here."

They spent the rest of the afternoon doing just that.

HALF AN HOUR BEFORE CLOSING, Allie and Lydia were pivoting slowly and admiring their work when the door opened. In swept Caroline Welch, Allie's friend and Eve's boss. Her straight hair only knew how to fall neatly in place, and she wore a capri pants outfit that was both casual and smartly pulled together. No matter the occasion, she was always impeccably dressed while exuding the quiet confidence of one too wealthy to have to dress to impress. In addition to brokering real estate deals for some high-ticket oceanfront properties, her office managed a number of rental properties in the tourist town of Pine Harbor and neighboring picturesque towns. So seemingly perfect a woman might have been easy to dislike if she weren't so darned kind. They'd been friends since kindergarten, and Allie adored her.

"Caroline!"

Lydia smiled at Caroline then returned to the counter and busied herself organizing the perfectly organized shelves.

After the usual warm preliminaries, Caroline got to the point. "I ran into Decker Wilmington just now."

"Oh. How's Decker?" Allie didn't actually care, especially since she'd just seen him at the wedding a few days before. But it seemed like the appropriate thing to say.

Caroline smiled. It was subtle, but having known Caroline since their school days, Allie knew it was as close to a smirk as Caroline got. She frowned for a moment. "He heard you were selling the Gallery."

Allie slowly blinked. "What? No!"

Caroline looked even more concerned. "Don't get

me wrong. I'm here for you if you ever want to sell. But I just couldn't believe—"

"No. I'm not selling. Why would Decker think that?"

Caroline exhaled, seeming truly relieved. "I'm sorry. Would you like to go sit down?"

Allie realized she should have been the one to suggest it. "Sure. Let's go to the back room. I'll make you some coffee." She was about to ask Lydia to cover for her, but Lydia was a step ahead of her. She gave Allie a nod that said she had the shop covered.

A few minutes later, Allie set down two coffees. Caroline took a sip. "That view never gets old. This is my favorite part of Pine Harbor, people going about the day's business, not so differently from the way they have done year after year."

Allie followed her gaze and knew just what she meant. Caroline handled some pretty exclusive properties, but the view from Allie's back window revealed Pine Harbor's true heart and soul. Out there, behind touristy storefronts and umbrellaed outdoor cafes, fishing boats pulled up to the dock, and box trucks parked and stacked crates of supplies. It was the down-to-earth business that kept Pine Harbor humming. In her small way, Allie's shop was a part of it all.

Caroline set down her mug. "What's going on?"

"I take it you weren't at the wedding."

"No. My father's caretaker was sick, so I spent the weekend at his place. But I should tell you, I don't have to ask how it went. And I've seen the video."

Allie leaned back and blew air through her lips. "I couldn't do it. I couldn't marry him. And I couldn't lie and say that I would. Although it would have been easier. But I couldn't stand there, look into his eyes, and just lie—then lie to everyone else."

If Allie could bottle the look on Caroline's face, she would. Straightforward compassion without pity was just what she needed.

"You don't have to justify what you did. I once had an offer of marriage myself that I had to turn down. Although I didn't have an audience. What was Justin thinking? Looking back, I shouldn't have accepted the second proposal, but you know what they say about hindsight."

"It sucks?" Allie nodded.

Caroline let out a rueful chuckle. A few years back, she'd gone through an ugly divorce. She'd gotten through it with a lot of talks with Allie and a few bottles of wine. "There's nothing like money to keep a couple together. He hated that I was the one making it, but he was too deeply in love—with my money—to let go."

With a hint of a smile, Allie said, "He seemed like such a nice young man."

Caroline sighed and shook her head. "I suppose I was lucky. The guy was a jerk, so no one worried about choosing sides."

That was putting it mildly. Caroline barely talked about it, but Allie knew he hit her once. It was three months into their marriage. After that, Caroline moved out, and that was the end. In the aftermath, she confided in Allie that he'd wept and begged her to forgive him. She told him she would, but she would never forget. From there, she lifted her chin and proceeded to build her own life. Seeing her strength both endeared her to Allie and inspired Allie to strive for such strength.

Caroline looked frankly at her. "We are not going to let them do this to you."

Allie shrugged. "I don't even know who *they* are, and I'm still stuck on why. It was a proposal, not a murder."

Caroline looked even angrier than Allie. "I've only heard bits and pieces." She looked at the door to the shop. "I take it business has been slow."

Allie swallowed back unexpected emotion. She'd always been taught not to talk about money. The truth was that she could make it through two, maybe three months before things grew dire. She was already feeling the pressure, but she couldn't admit it. "We get some tourists now and then."

Caroline gave Allie's wrist a squeeze. "This is going to end. I promise."

"Thanks, Caroline." Allie shook her head, too moved to get out more than that.

"Shh! I'll do some digging around. You just take care of you." She gave Allie a strong, no-nonsense look and got up. "Well, I've got work to do." She smiled brightly. "Have you been outside? It's gorgeous! Go take a walk. It'll help clear your head."

Lydia turned the sign over to the side that read Closed, then she unlocked the door to let Caroline out. "Would you like to go get some ice cream or something?" she asked Allie.

Allie was touched by Lydia's concern. "I'll be fine."

Lydia looked unconvinced, but Allie grinned and shooed her away.

DURING THE LULL BEFORE DINNER, Mel covered the bar while Theo sat at a table by the window with his laptop to knock out some work. But instead, he gazed out at the water.

Marco plopped down into a chair and chuckled when Theo flinched. "Getting a lot of work done?"

"More than you," Theo snapped back.

"Hey, I've cleaned the kitchen and prepped it for dinner, so don't look at me. I'm not the one staring out the window, daydreaming of Allie."

Theo narrowed his eyes, but the look that used to put fear into his brother only made Marco laugh.

Marco looked up and squinted. "What's that?"

Theo wouldn't fall for that old trick.

Unfazed, Marco pointed. "Are those...? Yes, those are fluffy thought bubbles with little hearts floating over your head. Oh, and what's that? Allie's name is in them."

Theo leaned forward. "There are times when you leave me speechless. Now's not one of those times, so shut up."

Marco burst out laughing. "Come on. I'm just kidding. Except for the part where you need to do something about it."

"Thanks, Marco, but I can take it from here."

"Of course you can. That's why you're staring out the window with that lovesick puppy look on your face." Marco leaned back, eyes twinkling, and folded his arms.

"You're a real smart-ass, you know."

Marco grinned. "Thank you." He got up. "I've got to get back to work." He turned then turned back. "One more thing."

Theo waited. *This is bound to be good.*

"Call her. Ask her out. You're welcome." He headed back to the kitchen.

What ticked Theo off most was that Marco was right. He'd never been like this over a woman before. That was because Allie was different.

THEO WALKED over to the bar and leaned over to Marco. "Be careful what you ask for. I'm taking the evening off. Can you manage?"

Marco smirked. "Can I manage? Yeah, Mel's here. Wednesdays aren't usually busy. Go on. We'll be fine."

Halfway into town, Theo realized he should have called. That was Marco's influence. Marco never thought two minutes ahead, but Theo was a planner, at least usually. He'd had to be. On the other hand, maybe not calling was better. If it seemed casual and unplanned, there might be less pressure. He wasn't sure who he was worried about, Allie or himself. Neither of them needed pressure at the moment. So they would take it slowly and see where it went.

He parked and took the long way around to the Gallery entrance. For some reason, knocking on the back door seemed presumptuous, so he went to the front. When he got there, the lights were dim, and the door was locked. *Great.* So he went around to the back, which he could have done to begin with. But he seemed determined to make everything more complicated where Allie was concerned. Before turning the corner, he heard voices and stopped.

ELEVEN

Lydia left for the day, and Allie was not far behind her. She decided to follow Caroline's advice. An evening walk sounded perfect. Maybe she would even go nuts and have some fish and chips at the dockside crab shack.

The front door to the Gallery rattled. Allie muttered, "Eight hours without a customer, and now that I'm closed, you decide to go shopping?" But she had no room to complain, the way business had been. So she went to the door, but no one was there. She unlocked it and looked both ways, but whoever it was was gone. She locked the shop door, grabbed her purse on her way out, and locked the back door.

"Hi, Allie."

Startled, Allie practically jumped. "Decker? What are you doing back here?"

He stepped forward from the telephone pole he'd been leaning against. "Nice place you've got here."

She frowned. "Thanks." He had seen it before, many times.

"The view's not bad either."

"I know. You can't beat a harbor view." He was acting a little weird, even for Decker. "Is everything okay?"

"Yes. Great, actually. The business is growing."

"That's great." She glanced toward the alley. "Well, have a good evening." She started to walk.

"We're going to be neighbors."

"Oh?" Allie stopped and tried not to grimace, but having Decker as a neighbor was anything but good news.

"I bought Loring's Toy Store. The closing's not for a couple of weeks, but I stopped by for another look."

"I didn't know they were selling." Loring's had been there since before Allie was born. It was a town institution. Mr. and Mrs. Loring were getting on in years, but Allie had never imagined they would sell.

Decker moved closer. "Yeah, well, they had to. Business was slow. Kids don't want those old-fashioned toys. It's all about video games, and they didn't keep up."

Allie felt terrible. She'd known the Lorings since she was a kid, and they ran into each other a few times a week. They would usually stop and chat. She had no idea they'd been struggling. How awful for them, especially at that point in their lives. She wished she had been able to help them somehow. It wasn't as though she was in any position to help them financially, but she might have at least been there to lean on.

Decker worked his way closer until he loomed over her. "You know, you ought to learn from their mistake. They hung on too long. If they'd sold sooner, they might have been able to walk away with something. But now they'll be lucky to walk away with some spare change."

Allie didn't think they would appreciate Decker broadcasting their financial status around town, but that was Decker. She folded her arms. "I'm sorry to hear that." She glanced toward the parking lot. "Well, I'll leave you to it. Good night, Decker."

He caught her by the arm as she started to leave. "Allie, I'd hate to see you go the way of the Lorings."

Allie looked down at her arm and eased it free. "I'll be fine." But she wasn't. She felt alone and increasingly uncomfortable.

"Allie, there you are!" Theo grinned and strode toward her. "I went to the front, but I guess I just missed you." He smiled and reached his hand out to Decker. "Theo Silva."

Nonplussed, Decker went through the motions, but a scowl slowly formed. "Decker Wilmington."

Allie realized it must have been Theo at her shop door minutes ago. She had no idea why he was here, but she was relieved to see him. Decker had never acted like that before. He was making her very uneasy.

Theo said, "Allie, I need your advice. Have you got a minute?"

"Sure."

She started for her door, but Theo said, "Actually, it might take a while. Why don't you let me buy you dinner?"

Allie was puzzled, but leaving with Theo was a far better prospect than staying with Decker, so she agreed.

"Nice to meet you, Decker." Without waiting for Decker's response, Theo turned to Allie and gestured toward the front of the building. They left Decker behind.

When they got to the sidewalk and rounded the corner, Theo stopped. "Sorry if I seemed pushy. I didn't like the way he was standing over you. It didn't look... comfortable for you."

"It wasn't. I'm glad you showed up." Allie hesitated then said, "So that was you at the shop door?"

He nodded.

"I'm sorry. If I'd known it was you—"

"No, that's fine. I was coming around to the back door when I saw you."

"I don't know what that was about. Decker's weird, but he's never been scary weird."

Theo ran his fingers through his hair. "I didn't feel right leaving you alone with him lurking outside your door. I hope you don't mind. Dinner was just an excuse to get you away from him."

"Oh." Allie tried to hide her disappointment.

Theo shut his eyes and exhaled. "That's not what I meant. I want to have dinner—with you. I just don't want you to feel obligated."

Allie couldn't hide her confusion. *Is he just being kind? Is this pity?*

Theo rolled his eyes in disgust. "I'm an idiot. I came here to ask you out, which I've completely screwed up." An insecure look flashed over his face.

Allie smiled. "I would love to have dinner with you."

He exhaled with apparent relief, which warmed Allie's heart.

"Good. Shall we?" He gestured toward the pier, and they walked and discussed their choice of restaurants.

IT DIDN'T TAKE LONG for them to forget the unpleasantness that had started the evening. Even lulls in the conversation were easy and comfortable. It was the kind of warm summer evening that made it easy to sit back in an outdoor cafe and listen to the water lap against the pier. There were times when it felt like they belonged like that, together with no further purpose beyond enjoying each other's company. But then Theo would smile, and it would fill her with wonder at how something as simple as that could make her heart swell. It wasn't just how he looked, although he was attractive. But she often leaned forward in anticipation for what he might say next. She loved how his mind worked, even when she didn't agree with him. That was half of the fun—disagreeing with him then going down the path of his thought processes. But then in a moment, he would look into her eyes, and she'd forget everything except how she felt right then.

After dinner, they went for a leisurely stroll and eventually wound up back at Allie's. She caught Theo surreptitiously looking around for any sign of Decker, but he was gone.

"I'm glad we did this."

"So am I."

There it was again, that electrical silence that made Allie feel as though sparks might explode in the air.

"Can I see you again?"

"Yes." *Every day. How 'bout now?*

"I shouldn't even ask this. It's so last minute. But tomorrow. Do you have plans?"

"Tomorrow's the Fourth of July."

He winced. "You've got plans."

Allie, Eve, and Lydia had planned a girls' night together. She couldn't bail on them, even for Theo. She nodded and wrinkled her face with regret. "I do."

"Of course you do. But I had to ask."

If he smiled like that much more, she might forget she had friends named Eve and Lydia and even what her own name was.

His eyebrows drew together. "Will you think less of me if I hate him, whoever he is?"

Allie laughed. It hadn't occurred to her that he would assume she had a date. "It's a girls' night with my friends. You can hate them if you like, but they don't really deserve it. They're really good friends." *Just don't ask me their names.*

"I'm glad you've got friends."

Allie realized they both had unabashed smiles on their faces. Then the smiles faded.

"Allie, I know you've had a lot going on, but I like being with you. I don't want to force something you're not ready for. It can be what you want it to be."

What I want it to be? At that moment, what she wanted it to be was something in the neighborhood of her jumping into his arms, wrapping her legs around him, and maybe ripping open his shirt, buttons flying. With her luck, one would land in her eye. Her saner self knew that she couldn't just act on her pheromone-induced impulses. He was right. She needed some time.

With conflicting emotions ricocheting in her brain, the best she could come up with was "Okay."

Okay? No one says just okay. When Romeo stood at Juliet's balcony and said, "O, speak again, bright angel," did she say okay? When Lancelot sang, "C'est moi, let's be lusty in May," did Guinevere say okay? When Jack said, "Hey, girl, don't jump off the Titanic," did Rose say okay? No!

Theo touched her shoulder gently and kissed her on the cheek. "I'll call you."

"Okay."

TWELVE

"Heads up, ladies. The tequila has arrived!" Kim pushed Allie's back door open with her hip and walked in with a box of clinking bottles and a bag of crushed ice threatening to spill over the side. She plopped it onto the counter with a grunt and headed back to her car.

"Need some help?" Lydia bounded out after her without waiting for an answer.

Eve and Allie unloaded the box of tequila, limeade, bar salt, and the largest margarita glasses Allie had ever seen.

"These aren't glasses. They're punch bowls."

Eve glanced at the door Lydia had just bounded through. "I've given her strict instructions. No alcohol."

Allie said, "Lydia's one of the most responsible high school seniors I know. I wouldn't worry."

"I don't—at least not when I'm with her." She leaned her palms on the counter and sighed. "But by this point, it's pretty much out of my hands. She'll make her own choices, whether I like them or not. I can only hope that she'll hear my voice in her head nagging, 'Don't do it!' Whatever *it* is."

They watched Kim and Lydia laugh on their way from the car.

Allie said, "She's amazing, you know."

Eve beamed. "I know. How did that happen?"

Kim entered, singing, "Tequila." The party had started. She held up her hands. "Okay, listen up! We're each taking turns doing the Pee-wee Herman 'Tequila' dance."

Lydia squinted. "The what?"

Kim said, "This is why your mom bought you a phone. Look it up later. For now... you can dance like your favorite *Bob's Burgers* character."

Lydia's face brightened. "Oh, okay! I'll be Tina!"

While they each took a turn, the others held up scores written on cocktail napkins. That was followed by Kim's version of charades, in which they split into teams and enacted a famous movie dance scene while the others guessed what it was. But Eve put an end to the game. "You can run and jump like you're in *Dirty Dancing*, but I'm not going to catch you."

They eventually collapsed into the Adirondack chairs on Allie's patio. Kim glanced inside and leaped from her chair. "Caroline's here!"

Having come straight from some swanky cocktail party, Caroline kicked off her heels as soon as she walked through the door. The whir of the blender drowned out most of their hellos as Kim wasted no time getting a drink into Caroline's hand. The five chairs and ottomans were a tight fit on Allie's tiny patio, but no one seemed to care. They had all been friends too long to have any pretenses. They were there to have fun—too much fun to notice if someone had to climb over outstretched legs and dodge drinks to make trips to the bathroom.

Caroline checked her watch. "Fifteen minutes until fireworks—time to take inventory." No one recalled when the tradition began, but whenever they got together as a group, they went around and answered a two-item questionnaire: "How's work?" and "How's your love life?" The first question got the shortest answers. The second often kept them busy well into the night.

Allie said, "You've got to be kidding. Fifteen minutes? That's three minutes apiece."

Kim took a sip of her drink. "And your three minutes is practically up. Sorry." She shrugged.

Caroline said, "I'll be quick. Work's a ten, and the rest is like tennis. Love equals zero." She laughed and touched her index finger and thumb to form a zero. She nodded toward it and added, "It's a visual aid. I figured after a couple of Kim's margaritas, you'd need it."

Kim leaned away in mock offense. "Apparently, I didn't make them strong enough, or you wouldn't care if you were understood." Kim looked around. "Lydia!"

Startled, Lydia looked up from her crocheting.

Kim said, "Wild child, it's your turn. How's work?" She leaned over and covered her mouth while she pointed at Allie. "Careful. Your boss is sitting right there." She returned to normal volume. "And how's your love life?" She lowered her voice again when she said, "Mom's here too. Dang! This is no fun!"

Lydia pushed her glasses up. "Work is great. Love my boss."

Kim spoke into a cough. "Suck-up."

Lydia smiled and added, "As for my love life... let's just say I get more recruitment letters from convents than colleges."

Eve said, "Let's keep it that way."

Lydia folded her arms and tilted her head inquisitively. "Mom, it's your turn."

"Work is great." She glanced at Caroline. "I mean it. And my love life is... perfect."

Kim hugged a throw pillow and leaned forward eagerly. "Really?"

At the same time, Lydia covered her ears. "I don't want to know."

Eve watched her, amused. "It's perfect because there is no man. There's just me in control of my life."

"Good for you." Caroline lifted her glass. "Here's to independence—for women as well as our country!"

Allie took a sip of her drink. "Way to bring it back to the Fourth of July."

Lydia said, "Wait, Allie didn't have a turn."

Allie narrowed her eyes at Kim. "Someone told me I'd used up my time. But short version: work is... fine." She and Caroline exchanged looks. It was anything but. "And my love life... just check social media—hashtag frigid fiancée."

That brought the room down. Kim rescued the moment. "There is someone new on the horizon—for Allie, not me."

Allie's eyes sparkled.

Kim prompted. "And his name is...?"

Allie smiled and hesitantly said, "Theo."

Kim added, "Silva."

Lydia chimed in. "Oh! As in Silva Brothers, that

new place down the road. I go to school with his brother. He's hot!"

Caroline turned to Allie. "Good for you."

Allie couldn't seem to stop grinning, but a sudden thought remedied that. "But that's just between us. I don't need to fuel any more gossip."

"Everyone raise your right hand." Kim looked serious if not quite sober. "Not a word to anyone." She waited then said sternly, "Repeat it."

Lydia said, "To whom? You just said—"

Kim interrupted, "I meant repeat it to me."

They said obediently, "Not a word to anyone."

As if in punctuation, the fireworks began with a boom.

AFTER A TEQUILA-INFUSED DISCUSSION about the logistics of watching one another safely on their way, Lydia declared that none of the adults would be driving. She would drive them all home. Stunned by her authoritative stance, they all had to agree that she was right.

Allie walked them to the car, where Kim made a hard landing in the back seat.

"Aw, Allie, you didn't need to escort us. Now who'll escort you?"

Impressed that Kim could still form coherent thoughts, Allie said, "I'll be fine. Go home. Take some aspirin. Drink some water. Happy Fourth!"

They drove off, and Allie stepped out of the bright lights of the municipal parking lot and into the shadowy alley that led to her door. Always acutely aware of her surroundings, she heard footsteps and a thud and glanced back, keys firmly arranged between her fingers as she formed a fist. But what she saw didn't pose any danger except to her heart. She'd had a few margaritas, so she didn't want to trust her first impression. A couple stood next to a truck and shifted position, bringing them into the light. It was Theo. And he was with a woman—the lavender-dressed date from the wedding. She leaned her back against a truck, and they kissed. It wasn't a peck on the cheek like the one he'd given Allie but a real face-sucking, spit-swapping kiss. Theo put his hands on her waist and guided her into the truck. *Is that his truck?* She'd never seen it. But the purple-dress girl looked quite at home.

Allie turned and walked away.

Earlier that evening

Theo locked the bar door. "We're officially closed! Happy Fourth of July!" The big fireworks display was in Pine Harbor. With everyone headed there, Theo and Marco had decided to give in and enjoy a rare evening off.

Marco hung up his apron. "I just need a minute to change."

Theo chimed in. "Me too."

Mel sat at the bar. "Don't mind me." She lifted her glass. "My friend Jack will keep me company."

Theo followed Marco upstairs to their apartment. "So Mel's coming along?"

"Yeah." Marco shrugged. It was no big deal for him, but Theo didn't agree.

"Okay, but she's your date."

Marco frowned. "Date? It's just fireworks. Relax."

Theo went to his room. Maybe Marco was right. He was making too much out of it. But Mel wasn't quite picking up the right signals. She was a great server, and she could tend bar like a pro. But as far as the two of them went, it was not going to happen. If he had his way, he would be with Allie. But she had other plans. He was glad she would be having a good time with her friends. She needed them at the moment, more than ever. And Theo could wait. He was playing the long game. But he still wished she could be with him that night.

The dockside bar was crowded, but it had the best view of the fireworks. After an hour, one barstool was vacated, so the three of them took turns sitting until Marco abandoned them. Despite the daggers Theo shot from his eyes, Marco joined some school friends he'd run into.

When the fireworks were over, Theo and Mel lingered awhile and talked shop with the bar owner until most of the crowd had dissipated. Theo hadn't paid much attention to how much Mel had been drinking until it was time to stand up. She careened into him, so he put his arm around her and hoisted her back to a standing position. With a few stumbles, they made it to the parking lot.

"My car's over..." She squinted and looked in the other direction. "I thought I parked there. No, there it is." She headed for it, but Theo hooked his arm about her. She spun back toward him and fell into his arms, lifting her eyes to meet his.

"I'm driving. My truck's over here."

Mel said, "I love a man who takes charge."

When they arrived at the truck, Mel reached for the truck door to steady herself then pivoted around, facing him. Theo gazed down at her. "I can't open the door. You're leaning on it."

"Oops. I'll just lean on you." And she did. She slipped her arms about his neck and pressed herself against him.

Marco will pay for this. "Come on, Mel. Time to go home."

She looked into his eyes. "Whose home? Your place or mine?"

Before he could answer, she kissed him. He pulled back, but she practically had a vice grip on his neck. Theo managed to extricate himself from her grasp. It was probably seconds, but those seconds felt like minutes—really long ones.

Fortunately, she passed out and drooled the whole way home. She was only half-conscious when he helped her inside. He didn't take a chance on venturing into her bedroom but instead left her on her couch, snoring.

ALLIE WOKE up with mascara tear stains on her cheeks. She moaned and muttered, "I hate men." She looked at the clock on her phone. "Ugh. I hate clocks." Then she remembered the shop was closed for the holiday. She pulled the covers back over her head and slept another two hours.

She woke to her phone's ringtone. "Hello?"

"Allie, it's Theo."

Allie sat up.

"Hello, Allie?"

She pressed the red button without saying a word. "Crap. Crap, crap, crap, crap, crap." She fell back onto her pillow and stared at the ceiling. "Men. I hate you. All of you." But her hate turned to sadness then to self-loathing.

How could you let this happen? Wasn't Justin enough? You couldn't just do what any sane woman would do and take time to heal? Nope. You had to walk into the men's room and fall in love. Crap. Ew. I probably shouldn't say that right after the men's room. Or maybe it's fitting.

Allie steeled herself. She was not going to cry. She'd only met the guy, really. He didn't deserve her tears. She took in a deep breath. *It never happened. I'll just unlock my mental diary and rip out the Theo pages like it never happened.* She took another deep breath. Then her hands got involved like a yoga instructor's, slowly in, hands floating up... and out, hands floating down. She rested her hands on her knees and relaxed her shoulders. Almost singing, she said, "And we are fine."

Serenely, she added, "And we hate men."

Theo tried calling a couple more times. She ignored him. He could go call purple-dress girl and kiss her. *Have at it, buddy. Or should I say, butt-y.* Realizing she'd regressed to a petulant four-year-old, she declared, "I need to go out."

She picked up her phone. Kim answered with less than her usual cheer and a voice that had dropped a few steps in pitch.

"Kim. Diner breakfast. Twenty minutes."

Her answer came slowly. "Uh, sure."

THIRTY MINUTES LATER, they sat in a booth with large plates of eggs, bacon, hash browns, and toast—along with Allie's coffee, diet soda, and two glasses of water. "I need to rehydrate," she'd explained to the server, who cast a blank look before leaving. She turned back to Kim without missing a beat. "The thing is, he was really convincing. Everyone within a sixty-mile radius who knows Justin now hates me—except Theo. He liked—me. I thought. I guess he likes Purple Dress more. I'm pathetic."

Kim was now fully awake and impressively stern. "Do not do that."

Allie set down the toast she was just about to shove into her mouth. "Do what?"

"Make it your fault when guys do stupid things."

That stopped Allie while she considered. "Well, I let him."

Exasperated, Kim asked, "Let him do what?"

Allie shrugged.

"Be nice to you? Tell you that he wanted to spend time with you? Wow. You're right. This is all your fault." She smirked at Allie.

Allie's mouth turned up at the corner. "Okay, maybe not. But I let myself open up and be vulnerable to him."

Kim's sarcasm faded. "I know. And that's the part that sucks because you can't avoid it. It's like a rite of passage with love. There's that moment—like bungee jumping—when you have to decide whether to turn back or just let go and jump."

Allie stared at her coffee. "An Icarus moment."

"Huh?"

"Greek mythology. Icarus and his father were imprisoned on Crete."

"Concrete? Sounds painful."

Allie smiled patiently. "No, Crete, a Greek island."

"Oh, boo-hoo, trapped on a Greek island. Want to talk trapped? Try four years at Vassar. Oh, the school's great, but you'll notice Edna St. Vincent Millay never wrote any poems about Poughkeepsie."

Allie continued, "So his father made two sets of wings so they could escape. The plan was to jump off a cliff and fly from the island."

"I could have jumped into the Hudson," Kim said while she carefully lifted the foil corner on a small pack of jelly. "Don't think I wasn't tempted."

"But the feathers were held on by wax, so Icarus's father told him not to fly too high, or the wings would melt."

"I wish my butter would. Look at this. Globs of hard butter on toast. I don't care. I'm too hungry." Kim took a big bite. "Mm... you know, this actually tastes pretty good."

Allie's eyes widened. "My point is—"

"Oh, yeah. What were we talking about?"

Allie's voice came out louder than she'd intended. "My love life!"

Three people in the next booth turned to look. Allie stared back like a deer into headlights until they turned around, then she lowered her voice. "My point is that I flew too close to the sun."

Kim studied her with a deeply creased brow. "And what's Theo? A sun god?" She wrinkled her nose. "Don't get me wrong. The guy's hot, but—oh! I get it. He's hot, and you flew too close, so your wings melted. Is that a euphemism for panties?"

Allie stared for a moment then gave up. "So... what's new with you?"

THIRTEEN

WHEN THEY GOT BACK to Allie's, they found Theo leaning against the door, waiting. Allie stopped, and Kim, who was texting, bumped into her.

Theo straightened his posture and asked, "Is everything okay? You weren't answering your phone.

Allie looked straight at him, too stunned to show any emotion. "Yeah, I'm fine."

His concerned expression shifted to confusion. "Are you sure?"

Allie kept her composure. "This isn't a good time to talk."

"Okay." His gaze shifted to Kim, who scowled.

He stepped away from the door but turned back to Allie. "I can see something's wrong. Can I help?"

Kim glared. "Oh, you've done enough."

"What?"

When Kim failed to answer, he turned to Allie.

She said, "Let's not do this now. I've got to go." She glanced at Kim, expecting her to follow, but Kim tilted her head toward the door as if to say, *You go inside. I got this.* Allie might have stayed to fight the battle if she hadn't been on the verge of an ugly cry. She was not about to let Theo see that. She had a scintilla of pride left.

THEO RAN his fingers through his hair, looking lost. "Kim, what happened?"

"What happened? Last night, you were tongue mining your waitress's throat. I'll bet that's a renewable resource."

"Oh."

"Yeah. Oh." Kim turned, but Theo rushed to her.

"Wait. It's not what you think."

"It never is, is it?" She let out a sound of disgust and pointed at him. "Allie is my friend. Do not. Mess. With her."

It would have been a formidable warning if her earring hadn't fallen and, with impressive reflexes, been caught by Theo. He handed it back to her, and she sheepishly thanked him.

Remembering her anger, she muttered, "Just leave Allie alone," and she walked away.

Theo watched her leave then returned to Allie's front stoop. He thought about knocking on the door until she answered, but he didn't want to make a scene. She'd had enough scenes for one week. Instead, he sat down on the stoop and thought. He couldn't blame her for being upset. Even though what they had was new, it was something special—or the beginnings of it. They hadn't discussed it and had no exclusive agreement. But what they shared was already palpable and needed to be handled with care. He stared at the ground. *What can I do?* She barely knew him—not enough to be able to trust him. And it would take some trust to move forward.

He shook his head and stood up. It was no use. He walked away.

Then he stopped and walked back. Yes, it was hopeless, but he still had to try. He pulled out his phone. Calling hadn't worked. At least if he texted, she would get the message. He knew she would delete it, but there was a chance she might read it out of curiosity first.

I know how it must have looked. He backspaced and deleted the whole sentence.

Allie, if you'd give me a chance, I think I could fall

in love with you. "No. Bring it down a notch," he muttered. He deleted it all except *Allie.*

What you saw was me trying to get a drunk woman home. "No! That is not what you mean. She'll take that the wrong way." He thought about putting the phone away, but he deleted the message instead and gave it one more try.

Allie, Mel was drunk, and she kissed me. I didn't kiss her back. But I couldn't leave her alone in that condition, so I gave her a ride home. The truth is that the only woman I've wanted to kiss since I met you is you.

He pressed Send, then he winced. *What am I doing?* He waited. *What I'm doing is standing here like an idiot because I can't do anything else.*

The door didn't open. *Did you really think it would?* Theo shoved his hands into his pockets and walked away.

What was that? Please let it be the door. He didn't dare believe it, but he turned. She was in the doorway with those big brown eyes gripping his heart.

"Did you mean it?" she asked softly.

His answer could not have been more emphatic. "Yes! She was drunk. I was just trying to do the right thing."

Her wide eyes looked lost. "I mean the part about wanting to kiss me."

He felt a smile spread through his whole body then

rushed to her and pulled her into his arms. He looked fiercely into her eyes. "Yes." And he kissed her. Every bit of pent-up desire and frustration went into that kiss.

"Did I drop my keys over here?" Kim rounded the corner. "Oh!" She stopped.

Allie looked over Theo's shoulder at Kim.

In the silent language of friends, Kim got Allie's message. "Nope. Must have... oh, duh, here they are in my pocket. Gotta go!" She did a sharp about-face and scooted around the corner.

Theo and Allie looked at each other and laughed, then he spun her around in his arms and kissed her again.

THE NEXT MORNING, Marco was cleaning the soda guns when Theo walked in and set down a box. While Theo happily whistled and restocked the bar, Marco stared.

"Somebody's in a good mood." Marco lifted an eyebrow. "I know that mood. Someone's been checking the oil."

. Mel walked in, looked toward them without making eye contact, and continued to the dining area to refill the votive candles on each table. Theo glanced at her, then gave Marco a dismissive look and kept working.

With the equipment wiped down, Marco folded his arms and leaned against the counter, amused. As if he didn't already know, he asked, "So. How's Allie?" He grinned and watched for Theo's reaction.

As the morning progressed, Marco took every opportunity to give Theo a hard time about the budding relationship. Theo had given him plenty of flak for his way with the ladies. *So what?* He liked women, and women liked him. That was what Marco would call a win-win. Since the tables were turned, it was payback time.

The business was humming, and Theo was happy. As the lunch rush died down, Marco sat at a small corner table and pulled out his phone. While he was scrolling through his social media accounts, a burst of loud laughter drew his attention to a table nearby. A tall, well-dressed guy seemed to be holding court over three others. Marco returned his attention to his phone, but he couldn't help but hear bits and pieces of the nearby conversation. The phrase "frigid fiancée" caught Marco's attention. He kept his eyes on his phone and an ear on the conversation.

One guy said, "I can't believe someone uploaded it." More laughter came.

Not wanting to be too obvious, Marco didn't look,

but the next voice was higher. "No one knows who did it. I've asked."

After that, it was so quiet that Marco couldn't resist looking. The tall guy had a Jack Nicholson grin on his face.

The first guy said, "You're kidding."

Another asked, "You?"

The grinning guy nodded.

The second guy said, "Oh man, that was cold."

Marco got up and sauntered over to Theo, who was manning the bar. "When you get the check for table twelve, let me know who it is."

Without looking, Theo said, "Decker Wilmington. He's a local commercial real estate mogul. Old money. A-hole. Why?"

Marco prided himself on being too cool to overreact, but he leaned back in amazement. "Whoa, that was specific."

Theo lifted an eyebrow. "Yeah? Well, we met under unfortunate circumstances. We already had our *oh crap* moment when he walked in."

"Wow. I've got to pay better attention. What happened?"

"He was giving Allie a hard time. I stopped him." He added, "Nonviolently—not that that was my first choice."

Marco realized Theo wasn't kidding. When Mel

walked by on her way to the kitchen, Marco asked her to watch the bar for a minute, then he grabbed his brother's arm and led him into the kitchen.

"Promise me you'll just listen and not do anything stupid."

Theo looked at Marco as if he'd lost his mind. "No. What are you talking about?"

Judging from Theo's reaction already, Marco wished he'd waited until Decker was gone. *Too late now.* He eyed Theo and braced for his reaction. "Decker just told his crew out there that he uploaded the video."

Theo didn't move.

"Of Allie. The proposal."

After the news sank in, Theo let out a series of curses and lunged for the door. Marco leaned in with his shoulder and just managed to stop him, but there was enough of a scuffle to draw Mel's notice. She stuck her head inside the door. "Hey! We can hear you! Everything okay in here?"

Marco gave Theo a questioning look.

Theo nodded. "Yeah, we're fine."

He stayed put but continued to call Decker a number of names. Then he pulled out a twenty and gave it to Marco.

"What's this?"

"For the swear jar." Theo continued until he ran out of expletives for Decker.

While Theo caught his breath, Marco said, "Remember what they say. 'Revenge is a dish best served cold.'"

Theo fumed. "If I kill him, we could lose the bar."

"Not to mention your freedom, so... maybe scratch that off your to-do list."

"What a bastard."

"I think you used that one already." Marco's mouth turned up a little.

Theo's anger faded. "Allie. She should know."

"No, don't tell her." Marco could see it play out. "You're just trying to get things going with her. You don't want to be the bearer of bad tidings she'll never forget."

"She deserves to be told."

"By someone, not you."

Theo looked down, deep in thought. "Yeah, I get what you mean. It would hurt her, and I'd be the cause."

Marco nodded, relieved. But as Theo stared at him, Marco anticipated what was coming next and slowly shook his head. "No."

"Yes. Someone's got to tell her, and as you said, it shouldn't be me. So that leaves you."

Marco shook his head and held up his palms. "No. Not gonna happen."

Theo practically pleaded. "It's easy for you. You've got that Silva charm."

"Oh, no. Don't use that against me." Theo always brought up the "Silva charm" whenever he accused Marco of treating girls' hearts with careless abandon. It still touched a raw nerve. Marco never set out to hurt anyone. All he did was like girls. It was genuine. He couldn't know that they would get the wrong idea. Theo had told him his good looks and charm had to be used carefully—like a boxer whose hands were considered lethal weapons. *What bull. I like girls. They like me. What's the problem?*

Theo lowered his voice and used his most serious tone. "I don't ask much."

Marco wanted to laugh. "No, just every day— several times a day—for the last ten years."

"Think of Allie."

It was another slow day at the gallery, so Lydia pulled out her crocheting. Allie popped her head into the door from the back room. "Can you hold down the fort? I need to run to the store."

"No problem." Yeah, she could hold down the fort.

The "fort" was empty and had been all morning. Lydia returned her attention to crocheting. *Poor Allie.* It just wasn't fair that her business should suffer. Like any small town, there was gossip, but she'd never seen it carried to such extremes. She glanced at the French notebook on the counter and recited irregular verb conjugations while she crocheted. She was short a year for her college's foreign language requirement, so she was hoping to test out when she started college. She had just finished the third-person plurals when the shop door opened.

"Hello."

She looked up. *Marco Silva?* A high-pitched "Hi" came from her throat. Lydia felt herself blush. *Please don't let him notice that my face looks like a radish.*

Marco came close—very close—and asked in a low voice, "Is your boss around?"

Lydia glanced toward the back room, knowing no one was there. "No."

"Good."

Lydia squinted and pushed her glasses up her nose. *Good?*

"We need to talk."

We? "We do?" *This might be the most exciting thing to happen in my life—ever. Marco Silva—the coolest guy in my high school—has to talk? With me?* She knew she was not in his league. To say she was bookish was putting it mildly. She knew it and owned it. But sometimes she would look at the popular girls and wonder what it must be like to have guys like Marco stop and lean on the next locker to talk between classes. That was their normal. She met Marco's eyes. *This is not mine.*

"What do we need to talk about?" Lydia was so nervous that she wouldn't have been surprised if her voice had come out sounding more like a sheep bleat. She tried to slow down her breathing. It wasn't like she and Marco had never talked before. One time, they'd been partnered for a global history project. On that day, Miss Hubert was her favorite teacher. Oh, how they'd talked about exciting and personal things like the Silk Road and PowerPoint graphics. Yeah, they'd made a connection—in Lydia's daydreamy mind.

Marco leaned on the counter. Every now and then, Lydia managed to force her eyes to flit up to meet his, but each time she did, she went stupid. She couldn't think. Heck, she barely could move.

He looked intense, which was a great look for him. "I found out something. We—Theo and I—think Allie should know. But the news can't come from Theo, and she barely knows me. It would be best coming from someone who knows her, preferably a good friend. Like you."

"Me?" Lydia was intrigued, so much so that she

nearly felt like herself. She was actually able to look straight at Marco and still think. "What kind of something?"

He narrowed his eyes. "This can't go further than between you and me."

Lydia's eyebrows lifted. "Okay." *What is it? Sure, I could sit here all day, gazing at your lips, your manly patrician nose, and your wavy dark hair. Does that one Superman curl just cascade to your eyebrow on its own? And yes, I get lost in your eyes. But they're brown. It's very dark in there. But you've got me curious, so please just spit it out!*

He exhaled. "We found out who posted the wedding proposal video."

Lydia's eyes widened. "You're kidding!"

He leveled a serious look at her. "Do you know a guy named Decker?"

She gasped. Marco nodded to confirm it. "Decker Wilmington? He's the one? How do you know?"

Marco told Lydia everything.

She frowned. "And you want *me* to tell her?"

He gazed into her eyes, which under normal circumstances would have made her light-headed. The fact that she was still standing was a testament to her regard for her boss. The thought of bringing the bad news to Allie made her squirm. For support and sympathy, she was great. But bad-news delivery was best left to anyone else. "Why not you? You're the one who found out." She nodded enthusiastically. "It should be you."

Marco said, "I don't know her that well. It would be easier to take coming from someone she's comfortable with. So you would be perfect."

"Perfect for wielding a devastating blow? No, thank you." *But I don't mind if you want to keep staring like that—into my eyes. You can do that anytime. No appointment necessary.*

Marco heaved a deep sigh and confessed, "Theo sent me to tell her."

It took Lydia a moment to overcome her Marco-induced swooning and piece things together. She frowned. "What? You... you're..."

Marco's expression would have looked adorably boyish if she weren't so annoyed. He said what she had already deduced. "But when I saw you here, I thought it might be better..."

"If I did your dirty work."

"Yeah." He looked sincerely regretful.

"How typical!"

Marco looked insulted. "Typical?"

"That's just so... your type."

"My type?"

"You just saunter in here—"

"Saunter?"

"Yeah, and assume I'm so—" *Pathetic.* She regrouped. "So... pliable—"

"Pliable?"

"Yes, pliable! Stop repeating everything I say!"

"I'm not repeating everything you say."

She scoffed. "You just did it again!"

"I'm sorry. I didn't mean to." Marco's eyes widened. He looked almost afraid.

Lydia put her hands on the counter and leaned over it. "You can't just assume you can have your way —" She paused. "I don't mean—not *that* way, just your way in general—with girls like me."

"Girls like you? What does that mean?"

"Girls like me!" She shrugged as if it should be obvious. Her eyes darted about and settled on the items she'd set on the counter. *Girls who crochet and conjugate French verbs in their spare time.* When she glanced back at him, a small surge of satisfaction coursed through her. He was on the defensive. It was clear in his expression. She smiled inwardly. It felt good to be in control. And he deserved having the tables turned on him for once. She lifted her chin. "You know what? You don't deserve to tell her. You're too... you! You would just make it worse. *I'll* tell her!" *Oh, crap.* There went her triumph. He'd just gotten his way.

Marco held her gaze. It was pretty intense. Lydia

nearly lost her train of thought. Then he glanced at the door.

She lifted her hands. "Go ahead. You can go. You've done what you came for. You've gotten me to do what you didn't have the b—guts to do. Well, I do, and I'll take it from here."

"That's not what I came for!"

But it is. She stared at him with narrowing eyes.

Marco shoved his hair back, frustration showing on his face. "What kind of a jerk do you think I am?"

Lydia continued staring.

Marco's brown eyes softened. His wounded expression touched Lydia until she had to fight the urge to apologize. *How did he manage to turn things around? Again.* Those were some dangerous eyes. *Steady, girl. You're annoyed, remember? Really, really annoyed.*

Marco said simply, "You're right. I'll tell her."

Oh, wow. Would you stop doing that? Making me like you? She heaved a big sigh. "We'll tell her together." The words just came out. Marco's surprise couldn't come close to hers. But it made sense. It *would* be better coming from her. *So why do I even need Marco? For moral support? Strength in numbers? Because I like him in spite of it all? Maybe all of the above.*

Minutes later, while waiting for Allie, Lydia and

Marco stood at the counter, heads together, while Lydia taught Marco how to crochet. He was looking triumphant over his first one-inch chain when the back door opened. They both stood up straight and turned toward the door.

Allie stopped in the doorway that led to the shop. Lydia's mind raced with ways to break the news to her, while beside her Marco shoved the crochet needle and yarn under the counter.

Allie must have picked up on their apprehension. She asked softly, "What?"

Lydia said, "Let's go sit in the back. I'll make coffee."

"Why?" Allie was beyond suspicious.

Lydia took the keys from a hook on the wall. "I'll just lock up and set the 'Be Back At' clock for an hour."

"An hour?"

Lydia's eyes darted to Marco then Allie. "Half hour?"

Allie's voice sounded strained when she asked, "What's going on? Has somebody died?"

"No, nothing like that." Lydia nearly continued but stopped. "Let me lock up first." She was halfway to the shop door when it flew open, and Theo burst in.

"Theo?" Allie looked alarmed—for good reason. He was wild-eyed and frantic.

Marco drew his attention from Allie. "Who's minding the bar?"

"Mel."

Marco didn't look thrilled. "She can't manage the whole thing alone."

Theo gripped Allie's shoulders. "Are you okay? Genius over there had me convinced I shouldn't tell you. I'm sorry. I should have been here."

While Theo led a bewildered Allie to the back room. Marco turned to Lydia and whispered, "I gotta go. I can't leave Mel with the kitchen, bar, and dining room on her own."

Oh, great. Leave me here with these two. "Sure. Okay."

It was even more okay when Marco scanned the counter, grabbed a pen, and took Lydia's hand. In fact, the evening could have ended right there on a high note.

Marco said quietly, "Here's my cell. Call me when this train wreck is over." He rushed out while Lydia stared at her hand.

FOURTEEN

THEO LED Allie to a chair and pulled one up for himself. "You should have been here for what?" Allie asked Theo.

Theo's face blanched. He gave Lydia with a questioning look. She pursed her lips and shook her head slightly.

He winced. "I thought Marco told you."

"No one told me, but somebody had better tell me soon, because you're scaring me!"

Lydia lifted a finger. "I'll just go mind the shop while you two have a talk." She hurried off and gently closed the door behind her.

When Lydia was gone, Theo said, "I'm so sorry. I've botched this up royally."

Allie's impatience mounted. "I'm sure I'd agree—if you'd tell me what's going on!"

Theo blurted out, "It was Decker." When Allie's confusion didn't seem to subside, he added, "Decker recorded the proposal on his phone and uploaded it."

Allie couldn't speak for a long time. When she finally did, she asked, "Decker?"

Theo filled her in on the details of what Marco had heard.

She stared off into the distance while she processed the news. "Decker. What a jerk. What an absolute jerk. I mean, he's always been about as appealing as a sommelier's spit jar, but I kept trying to give him the benefit of the doubt."

"He didn't deserve it."

"Obviously not." Allie couldn't seem to stop shaking her head. "If my business hadn't suffered, I'd... well, probably swear, maybe at him directly, but I'd get over it, because life is too short. But this might ruin me. The shop is hanging on by a thread—no pun intended."

"Yeah, I've got to say I've seen small-town rumor mills in action, but Pine Harbor has really leveled up."

"My business is at stake, so if Decker wants to play hardball, I've got some photos."

"Of Decker?" Theo's eyes lit with curiosity.

"Yes." A thought made her panic. "Oh! No, not, uh, inappropriate photos. Just photos." In spite of it all, Allie couldn't help but smile. "Tenth grade science fair. We were partnered together for a project. We didn't win a thing, but my dad took lots of pictures. Decker's haircut was a science project all on its own." She leaned her head back in the chair and looked up toward the ceiling. "I should really post those on the internet."

"It's the least he deserves."

"But sadly, I won't." She turned toward Theo. "I couldn't be that mean." Looking into Theo's kind eyes seemed to lessen the pain. "Besides, the damage is done. I've recovered. Well, more or less. The shop might not. But to be honest, I still can't imagine how refusing Justin was enough to drive the whole town—and some tourists—away. I mean, gossip is one thing, but boycotting the Gallery seems over the top. Maybe it's just me... or the shop. Bad marketing. Maybe the concept has just run its course."

Theo shook his head. "Your work is too good, and you've got a great inventory of local artists' work and gifts. The Gallery captures the nostalgic spirit of this salty seaport and days gone by. It's everything tourists could want in a shop. I mean that in a good way!"

"Thanks, but you might be a little biased."

Theo's eyes twinkled. "I wouldn't let my feelings impair my flawless judgment."

"Of course not."

He squeezed her hand. She was getting used to his touch in the sense that she would never grow tired of it.

Theo stood. "Look, let's get out of here. A walk might clear our heads and put things into perspective."

Allie agreed. "I'll let Lydia know."

LYDIA STOOD by the door and stared at her watch until it clicked over to five, then she locked the shop door. With the shop so predictably empty and quiet, she'd had plenty of time to try to figure things out. She hadn't stood with her ear to the door while Allie and Theo talked through things, but she happened to overhear Allie's theory that the boycott was about more than the proposal video. It made sense. An entire community wouldn't have rallied behind Justin to such an extent. Sure, Justin was a nice guy—nice enough for sympathizers to avoid Allie for a day or two, but life had to go on at some point. But not even the tourists came in anymore. Lydia tried to work up a few theories, but she didn't have enough facts to support them.

She plopped her bag onto the counter and packed up her books and crocheting. Marco's crochet chain caught her eye, and she took out her phone. *Marco said to call him.* Lydia had proof of that on her hand. She studied his handwriting then got sidetracked musing about which soaps were least likely to remove ballpoint ink. She blew air through her lips. *Come on, Lydia. Ten digits. You can do it. Just dial.*

"Marco? It's Lydia."

"Hi." Glasses clinked in the background.

"You said to call, so..."

"Yeah. Look, they're here now."

"Allie and Theo?"

"Yeah." If a tone of voice could say "duh," his just had.

"Oh, okay. So..."

"I can't talk here. Want to meet somewhere?"

Her pulse quickened. "Uh, sure. Where?"

"How 'bout the diner around the corner from your shop?"

"Okay."

Marco said, "I'll be there in ten minutes."

"Okay." She would be there in two. *Calm down, girl. This is all about Allie and Theo.*

Rather than sit in a booth like a sad lump of aloneness, Lydia tidied up around the shop for seven minutes. That left one minute to walk to the diner, one to wait for a table in case it was busy, and one to look at her phone as if she were busy messaging someone.

Marco was early. She rounded the corner as he reached the diner from the opposite direction. He smiled and said, "Perfect timing."

They went in and sat down. Marco wasted no time

getting to the point. As they finished updating each other on what they had missed, Lydia's mood sank. She had outlived her purpose where he was concerned. There was nothing to add and no reason to continue.

Marco grinned. "What are we going to do about those two crazy kids in love?"

Lydia laughed. Although Marco could have read the menu to her, and she would probably have giggled like a lovestruck hyena. She cleared her throat and tried to calm down. "I think they'll be fine without us." *Brilliant. Now he won't need to talk to you ever again.* She pushed her glasses up. "But I'm worried about the Gallery. Did Allie mention to you that she thinks the drop in business is about something else besides Decker's video?"

"No, but I overheard them at the bar, trying to figure it out, but they couldn't."

Lydia shrugged. "Do you think it's just a coincidence?"

"Could be. But I don't know. It was so sudden. Something doesn't seem right."

Marco stared at his coffee. "People talk at bars. The more they drink, the louder they get. Maybe I can get somebody talking."

"Thanks." He didn't have to do that. After all, his brother and his business were fine without taking Allie's problem on.

As if reading her mind, Marco said, "Just between you and me, Theo really likes Allie. *A lot.* Helping her is important to him. And a happy Theo means less pressure on me."

"Really? Why?"

Marco told her Theo had raised him since he was eight. When he'd finished, the server stopped by to refill their coffees. Lydia noticed Marco got a much warmer smile than Lydia did.

"So, what about you?" he asked.

"Me?"

For some reason, her reaction amused him. "Yeah, you. What's your story?"

"Oh, it's just me and my mom. She works in the real estate office next door to the Gallery." Lydia didn't know what else to say.

"And...?"

"And what?" Lydia took a sip of her coffee, glanced around, then looked back at Marco. He hadn't moved.

"And what about you? What do you do in your spare time? Besides crocheting?"

When she hesitated to answer, he continued, "Are you going to college? If so, where? If not, what will you do—be a career shopgirl?"

Lydia cringed at how boring her life must look to him.

"In my spare time, I read books and go for walks. In

the fall, I'm going to Pine Harbor Community College. I'll keep working part-time at the Gallery while I'm in school. After that, I don't know. I guess I need to decide."

She couldn't hold his gaze, so she glanced away and then looked back at him. He grinned.

"What?"

"You're different."

Something deflated inside her. "Yeah, I'm aware."

Marco leaned back and gazed into her eyes. He really needed to be careful about that. He couldn't know the effect it had on her. He laughed. "I mean different in a good way. A lot of girls I know just talk about themselves, but you don't."

"No." She felt embarrassed. He'd cracked the code. She was different from all of the girls he knew in school —all the popular girls. *Like you couldn't tell from looking at me?*

"It's a good thing—being different."

Is it? Like a thin ribbon of light in a dark cave, hope seeped into her heart.

He said, "I'm different. I used to feel like I didn't fit in, then I stopped caring. People say things and think things, but you can't let it define you, you know?"

No. "Yeah." She nodded, as if she understood. He was so different—in a cool way that made people wonder what he was thinking. He didn't care what they thought, and that drew people to him—especially girls. Marco Silva was magnetic, while Lydia was the polar opposite.

Marco glanced at his watch. "Oh, man! I've got to get back to the bar before the dinner rush!" He reached into his pocket and pulled out a twenty. "I got this." He tossed it onto the table, flashed a grin, and raced out of the diner, leaving Lydia staring, fascinated.

FIFTEEN

A\LLIE OPENED ALL the windows in her apartment to let the sea breeze flow through the apartment. It was a glorious morning. She sat down by the street-side window to savor her coffee and take a pulse on how busy the traffic was before going downstairs to open the shop. While locals scurried to work or on errands, tourists strolled at a leisurely pace in the mid-morning sunlight. A woman and a teenaged girl stopped outside Allie's shop and admired the window display. Allie smiled. She and Lydia had spent an entire afternoon on that window—one of Allie's projects to fill the time they would ordinarily have spent ringing up customers.

"Let's come back after lunch," the teen said to the woman, whom Allie assumed was her mother.

"What's the name of this place?" Allie was tempted to call out the name from her window.

The mom read the sign. "Oh, the Gallery. That's the one."

The one—what?

The mother continued, "Oh, maybe you weren't there. I overheard the B&B owner talking with a man. It's not like they were whispering. I mean, I couldn't help but overhear. Anyway, this is the shop."

"The shop... what?" her daughter asked.

"There's a ringworm outbreak in there."

What? Allie wanted to scream out the window.

"Ew, gross! What's ringworm?"

"You know, I've heard of it, but I can't really remember. Anyway, the owner has it, and it's all over everything."

Allie's jaw dropped. *Ringworm?* She examined her hands. *I've got a little eczema on my hands, but... what the heck? Ringworm?*

A moment passed, then her daughter asked, "So there are, like, worms crawling all over the shop?"

"No, it's some sort of skin thing," her mother said, sounding impatient.

Her daughter gasped. "Oh, I think I saw that in a movie once. All your fingers and toes slough off, then your nose..."

Allie said, "That's leprosy."

The girl looked up as if she'd heard. Allie shrank into the shadows.

The mother looked deep in thought. "I don't think it's that. I just know we don't want it on us, so we'll steer clear of 'the Gallery.'" She used air quotes for the shop name, which really irked Allie.

Oh, come on! It's just athlete's foot, only not on your foot. Either way, we don't have it. And it's better than hoof-and-mouth disease, which you seem to have, you old bag!

Allie might have told them as much, but they left before she could stick her head out the window.

When she'd calmed down, she thought through what she'd overheard. *A guy is spreading that rumor? What guy?* That was an easy one. It had to be Decker. Allie glanced at her watch and headed downstairs to open the shop. As she came down the stairs, she heard persistent knocking on the front door of the shop. "Caroline?" Allie hurried to open the door for her.

Far from her usual unflappable self, Caroline rushed inside. "Someone's sabotaging my business!" She paced back and forth in front of the counter. "It happened yesterday at a showing."

"It?"

Allie watched Caroline with concern. Caroline's hands trembled, and her eyes were rimmed in red.

"I didn't know the homeowners well. I'd just visited the house once—gorgeous house—and it showed beautifully. They'd already moved out but left enough furniture to stage it. They came to the office the next day to do the paperwork to hire me as their real estate agent. I knew it would sell fast, and the commission was nice. So yesterday, I brought a couple to see it. We walked in, and there were cockroaches—huge ones—scurrying about in the kitchen. I thought—well, I didn't think at first. I just rushed my poor clients outside and assumed it was an unfortunate problem—not mine but the homeowners' problem."

"That's weird. We don't get many cockroaches here."

"I know. So today, I had a big open house. Stunning estate on a hill overlooking the harbor, fully renovated, pool, views to die for—big-ticket item. Big commission for me. If I sold it. So I scheduled an open house." She touched her forehead and moaned. "Thank god I got there early! It was such a perfect day. I put the open-house sign in the front yard, then I went to my car and got a cookie sheet and a package of chocolate chip cookie dough. When I got to the kitchen, same thing." Caroline stopped and shook her head.

"Cockroaches again?"

Caroline shuddered. "The kitchen was crawling with them—walls, sink, and cabinets. I left a handwritten note on the door that the open house was canceled. What else could I do? When I called the owners, they blamed it on me! Me! Like I brought them in with me in my purse!" She lowered her voice when she said, "I never liked that couple, but the house was amazing. Anyway, it's someone else's sale now. They fired me."

"I'm sorry, Caroline."

"At least it saved me the trouble of calling an exterminator and dealing with that. I hate bugs."

"I know," Allie offered sympathetically.

"Everyone knows it. I've always been squeamish around them—and worms. Remember biology?"

Allie did. Everyone in her class would have. "I still think it was mean the way Decker dropped that dissected worm down your shirt."

Caroline stopped moving. "Oh my gosh!"

Allie waited, increasingly curious.

"Do you think it was Decker?"

Allie was confused.

Caroline nodded and began to pace again. "What are the odds? Cockroaches two days in a row? It's not like we're in the Deep South or New York City."

"Decker? But why target you?"

"The more I think about it, the more it makes sense."

In a way, Allie could see it. She wouldn't put it past him, but she wasn't sure why he would do it. "I thought he did commercial real estate and you did residential properties. Why would he sabotage you? You're not really a threat to him."

Caroline would not be dissuaded. "He's known since high school biology that I hate bugs—seriously hate them."

Allie recalled her earlier incident with the mother and her daughter outside her window. "If it makes you feel any better, you're not alone. Decker's been spreading a rumor that I've got ringworm."

"Ringworm? Why ringworm? I mean, he could have come up with something that sounded a little more deadly—or less absurd."

"This is Decker we're talking about."

They both managed to laugh in spite of themselves.

Allie mulled it over then said, "He used to tease me about my hands."

"Why? What's wrong with your hands?"

"Oh, you know, I've always been allergic to everything. The school soap made my hands break out in a rash. He used to make fun of me."

Caroline shook her head. "What a charmer."

Allie frowned. "If he wanted to hurt me, it kind of makes sense. I still have a little eczema. It flares up now and then, especially when I'm stressed—like I've been since the wedding proposal. If people look at my hands, they might think this is ringworm."

Caroline mulled it over. "It still sounds ridiculous."

"But it worked. Look at this place. This is how it's been since the wedding."

Caroline's look of deep concentration relaxed. "So he knows I hate bugs and infests all my houses. And with you, it's your skin. But why would he want to hurt us so much?"

"He'd have to really hate us a lot. What have we ever done to him?"

After a few moments of thought, Caroline said, "What if it's not us but our businesses?"

Allie squinted, skeptical. "You think he has a burning desire to open an artsy gift shop—what with him being so artsy and all?"

Caroline chuckled.

The phone rang.

"Allie, it's Theo." She could hear the smile in his voice.

"Hi. How are you?"

"I miss you."

"Really?" She must have sounded different because Caroline lifted her eyebrows and smiled. Allie realized she was beaming. She pointed to the phone and mouthed, "Theo."

Caroline mouthed a sarcastic "No!" and stepped out to the patio.

Theo asked, "Any chance you could get away for a

coffee? I'm trapped here, but if you came to the brewpub, I might sweeten the deal with some lunch."

Allie looked through the door to her shop, which hadn't seen a customer in days. "Sure. Why not?" She thought of Caroline. "Can I bring a friend?"

"That depends."

"On what?"

"If it's a date, no, you can't."

Allie laughed. "No, it's my friend Caroline. I don't think you've met her."

"Sure, bring her along."

On the way over, Eve called. "We need to talk."

Fifteen minutes later, Theo led Eve and Lydia to Allie and Caroline's umbrellaed table in the outdoor seating area and took their drink orders. Before he went back to the bar, he gave Allie a smile that made her wish she'd come alone. A group gathering couldn't have been what Theo had envisioned when he called her, but he was good-natured about it.

As soon as he was gone, Lydia wasted no time. "Allie, my mother has something to tell you."

Eve said, "There's a rumor—"

Allie saved her the trouble. "That I've got ringworm?"

"Ringworm? No, something else. I keep forgetting the name. I think it's... toxic necrophilia."

"Mom! No! That's sex with dead people!"

Allie said dryly, "I do dead people?"

Caroline fought back a grin.

"Wait, I wrote it down." Eve pulled a piece of torn paper from her purse. "Toxic epidermal necrolysis."

Before Allie could ask what it was, Eve continued, "I ran into a friend from my book club who said she'd heard that you have it and the whole shop is infected."

"What?" Allie laughed, but it wasn't a happy laugh. The rumor was so outrageous that it was laughable. But its effect on her business was not.

Eve continued, "When she said your mother died of it—"

"My *mother*?"

"I had to call you."

Allie leaned back and stared at the table. "My mother's in Florida! My parents retired and moved to Miami."

"I know that, but someone else doesn't seem to."

Caroline shook her head. "Or someone knows it but wants to ruin Allie's business. And mine."

By the time they finished their drinks, Eve and Lydia were all up to speed.

Eve squinted and stared off to the distance, so deep in thought that she didn't hear Theo pull up a chair and join them.

"Mom?"

Eve turned to Lydia. "What, honey?"

"You've got that look on your face—the one when you're thinking about paying the bills or doing taxes."

Eve still seemed distracted. "No, I was thinking of something Mel said."

"Mel?" Allie tilted her head toward Theo.

He said, "My Mel?" He shut his eyes for a moment then rephrased it. "Not *my* Mel but *our* Mel—here at the bar."

Eve said, "Yeah. She stopped by the office to pick up a check."

Caroline explained, "I use her for catering gigs now and then." She looked at Theo. "She's very good. Hang on to that one."

But not literally. Allie worked to maintain a pleasant expression. There was nothing wrong with Mel, she reminded herself, except for her gift for insinuating herself into Theo's life. The girl had good taste. She would give her that.

Eve continued, "So, Mel stopped by the office on Friday. We were chatting, and she mentioned she'd just come from a meeting with Decker. He hired her for a party."

Caroline said dryly, "Oh, good! I can't wait to get home and check my mailbox for my invitation."

Eve laughed. "The thing is that he was running late, so while Mel was waiting, she heard him talking with someone about a new waterfront development. It sounded like a pretty big deal, so she asked if I'd heard anything about it. Small town. Word gets around. But I hadn't. Has anybody else?"

No one had, which seemed odd to Allie. Decker didn't do things in a small way, so if he made it sound like a big deal, it probably was. She thought out loud, "A big waterfront development."

Lydia leaned toward Allie. "Didn't you say he bought the toy store next door?"

Theo's eyes narrowed. "Yeah, we had a little run-in right after that. He was lurking outside Allie's shop."

Caroline's eyes widened, and she nodded. "And my office is next door to yours. That's three businesses in a row. He's got the toy store, and his rumor has pretty much killed the foot traffic to your store."

"And now he has sabotaged two of your open houses," Allie said.

Theo slapped his fist on the table. "That bastard."

"What?" Lydia glanced about, looking confused, then her face lit as the truth dawned on her. "He's after your property. He's trying to ruin your businesses so he can buy them up!"

Eve scowled. "And turn our quaint fishing village into some kind of carnival by the sea."

Theo flagged Mel down. "Tell us what you know about Decker."

SIXTEEN

Marco caught Lydia's attention and beckoned her to the bar. She slipped away and sat on a stool at the end. The rest of the bar was empty, except for a couple at the opposite end. Marco wiped his hands on a towel and leaned on the bar. "What's up with you guys at the table? It looks intense."

When Lydia finished explaining, Marco folded his arms. "Man, that Decker is some piece of work."

"I know."

"I can't say I'm surprised." He leaned closer. "He's been in here a few times. Orders us around like we're here to serve only him and no one else matters."

Lydia glanced over at the table. "Mel says he was talking about some presentation to the town's planning board. If they approve it, all that's left is to drive Allie and Caroline out of business so he can have their land, which means my mom will be out of a job—and we'll lose our apartment. We might have to leave Pine Harbor. Sometimes life sucks."

"Slow down. You don't know that."

"Maybe not, but I know Decker." A new thought came to mind. "Loring's Toy Store just closed—next to the Gallery. I just assumed they decided to retire. Now I realize he didn't just buy them out—he drove them out." She frowned. "I liked the Lorings. They used to give me lollipops."

Marco's eyes twinkled. "When was that? Last week?"

She narrowed her eyes. "No! When I was a kid."

Marco smiled, and Lydia forgot her annoyance.

He must have seen Theo approaching, because he started looking busy by wiping the bar. "The planning board could turn him down."

Lydia knew better. "No, he'll be impeccably dressed, which to the powers that be is almost as good as being smart—not to mention old school friends, greased palms, and calling in favors." She leaned back, defeated.

Marco leaned on the bar. "Would you really have to move?"

Lydia shrugged. "If my mom can't find work."

"But you don't know that for sure."

"Marco, we've got one stoplight. You can walk the

length of the town in ten minutes. There aren't many jobs on that ten-minute walk."

"Maybe Decker will blow the presentation."

"It's no use. It's a done deal. There's nothing we can do."

They contemplated their fates for a minute, then Marco's eyes brightened. "Unless..."

Lydia was too dejected to pay much attention to Marco's feeble effort to cheer her up. But he leaned closer. The light in his eyes took on a devious gleam.

"Unless what?"

Marco's mouth turned up at the corner. "I was just thinking about Decker's deck."

Eve walked by with the others. "Lydia, ready to go? I'll be by the door."

Thanks, Mom. Lydia gave Marco a helpless look. "Gotta go."

"I'll call you."

With that, Lydia's day was looking up, then it crashed just as quickly. "But you don't have my number." She glanced nervously at the door, where her mother pointed at her watch.

Marco said, "I should have it from when you called me. Just in case, text me on your way home so I'll have it."

"Okay. Bye."

Theo hung his apron on a hook and left Marco alone at the bar. "Be back later."

"Later when?"

"I've got my phone," Theo answered and left through the kitchen.

Marco muttered, "Objection. Nonresponsive."

Mel joined Marco at the end of the bar. "Where's he going?"

"Out."

Marco watched Mel gaze at Theo as he left through the back door. "Sometimes it's just not meant to be."

She grimaced. "I don't know what you're talking about."

Mel grabbed a rag and got busy wiping down tables while Marco pulled out his phone and read a text from Lydia.

ALLIE LEANED her head back on the headrest. "So, this is your truck." *Of course it's his truck.*

"Yeah. All mine since 2011."

For some reason, Allie felt nervous. *Some reason?* That reason had a name: Theo. They'd spent time together, and they'd even kissed. She reflected on that for a bit. But this almost felt like a date—a first date. "So, where are we going?"

A light came into his eyes and spread to his lips. "My favorite place."

"Which is...?"

"My place."

"I thought you lived over the bar."

"Yeah, for now. But I've got my eye on a small patch of land that's for sale. Want to see it?"

"Sure."

They pulled off the main road and followed a dirt road for half a mile until they got to a clearing. "This is it."

"It's nice." It was a meadow lined with trees, which could describe almost any plot of land in the state.

Theo laughed. "Yeah, just wait."

They got out of the truck, then he took her hand and led her through the trees.

At that point, Allie didn't care where he led her. Trees, meadow, swamp—it didn't really matter as long as she was with him. It was no longer open to discussion or to her inner musings. She liked Theo Silva—a lot.

Theo stopped. "Here we are." He hooked an arm about her waist then grinned. "Just a safety precaution. There's a steep drop-off."

She leaned closer and lifted her eyes. "I feel safer already."

He gazed at her. "The view up here is amazing." He leaned down and kissed her. "The view's not quite as good, but if you look through those trees..." He guided her over a few steps to a clearing.

Allie gasped. "Oh, wow! It's gorgeous!" All of Pine Harbor lay below. Half a dozen trawlers were docked in the harbor. Not far past them, scattered cutters and sloops glided along, looking like origami on the glistening blue stretching to the horizon. A wave of happiness washed over her.

"So you like it?"

"I do."

They stood arm-in-arm, looking out to the sea, and Allie was wholly content. Theo led her to a large boulder, where they sat.

"I come up here sometimes to think. I'm hoping to buy it." He looked down bashfully. "I'm almost there, so fingers crossed, no one buys it before I can. The owner's a regular at the bar. We've become friends. As a favor, he's promised me first refusal." Theo's eyes sparkled. "Although he might have been drunk at the time."

Their smiles faded, and a comfortable quiet settled.

After a long while, he said, "Allie, I don't know

what we are or what we're going to be, but I want to be friends."

She felt slightly rejected but wasn't sure if that was what he was doing. It sounded that way. She exhaled, evidently too loudly.

"Oh my gosh." He looked stunned. "Do you think I was... what do you think?"

"That you want to be friends?" One of the things about him she had loved from the start was how easy he was to talk to. *Except now.*

"I'm an idiot."

"No, not at all." *Just confusing.*

"Allie, I love it up here, and I wanted to share it with you."

"I love it too." *But I'm still confused.*

"I'm not making any sense, am I?"

She slowly shook her head. "Maybe?"

He shoved his hair back and looked around. "I feel like we've got something special."

She nodded.

He took her hands in his. "So I want you to know how I feel, and I want to take time."

Allie thought back but couldn't figure out where the signals had gotten crossed. "Did I do something to make you feel like I was moving too fast?"

His jaw didn't quite drop, but it looked close to it. "No! I am! I didn't want to scare you."

"How could you?" She wanted to laugh from relief, but he looked so tortured that she took pity on him. Then she suddenly got it. He didn't want to be Justin. She couldn't exactly say that.

"It's scary."

He looked worried. "What? Being with me?"

"Well, yeah, but not like you're thinking. It's scary feeling like this but not knowing for sure where it's going."

"Yes!" He got it. They got each other.

She smiled. It was their Icarus moment. How fitting to be up there on a hill.

Theo's eyes shone. "I just want you to be happy." He searched her eyes then kissed her.

Well, that's a good start. Enough talking. Let's go with this new plan. She just wanted his lips on hers and his hand on the back of her head where it was. She wanted him, not his friendship. Allie had enough friends. Her heart never pounded like that with her friends.

The kiss ended, and Theo leaned his forehead on hers. "Just to be clear, I don't want to be friends." His eyes were bright with amusement. "I want to do this." He kissed her again.

She said, "Okay, I think we're on the same page."

He kissed her a third time, a long, thorough one. "It's a very long book."

THEY SPENT THE AFTERNOON TOGETHER, talking and laughing. It was easy again. They'd crossed into a new unspoken agreement, a shared trust that they would go on the journey together, wherever it led. They had no need to rush and would take time to figure it out.

Theo looked at the horizon. "There's something I've wanted to say."

Allie waited. *Why do people say things like that?* It made her nervous. They'd been doing so well.

He went on. "I've been worried about your situation."

"My situation?"

"With your business—with Decker."

"I'll get through it. I'm a grown-up."

He smiled. "I know. But Decker's the kind of guy who doesn't play fair. Judging from his actions so far, I don't think he'll stop till he gets what he wants. So I want you to know I'll be there if you need me."

Allie wanted to say she didn't need any help, but she wasn't sure if that was true. She was sure she was strong, and she would fight Decker. She might lose, but she would do her best and find her way through what came next. "I don't need to be rescued."

"I didn't mean that. You'll be fine on your own. You're independent and smart."

He took a few moments to think—so many moments that Allie broke the silence. "You ran out of compliments, didn't you?" She smiled.

He laughed then continued, serious once more. "When I became Marco's guardian, I didn't have a clue what to do. All I knew was that I loved my brother, and I wouldn't let anyone split us up. I wasn't really equipped to provide a stable home, but the court needed proof that I was. Like you, I was strong."

Theo swallowed. "People stepped up to help— people I didn't even know I could ask. But they believed in us and wanted to keep us together almost as much as I did—enough to help us. Suddenly, we had a rent-free place to live. People went to court and vouched for my character. I had a job, and somebody said they would give me a job if my current job fell through. It all fell into place. Friends pitched in and made sure it could happen. We had a home and a future, and we were a family. You can't pay people back for something like that. It's worth too much. I knew then if I ever had the chance, I would be there for others."

He took her hands in his. "Let me be there for you. You might not need it, but I want you to know it."

Allie didn't know what to say, so she kissed him.

SEVENTEEN

LYDIA GRABBED her crocheting and sat down on her bed. Just as she'd gotten her three pillows comfortably arranged, her phone chimed. She didn't get a lot of text messages, especially so late at night. It was sad but true. When she saw that the text was from Marco, she dropped her crocheting.

Can we meet? it read.

She thought, *Sure, come on over. Climb the tree outside my window. I'll be waiting in bed.* Lydia imagined herself with one arm casually behind her head as she seductively lounged across her Disney princess bedspread in her Soffe shorts and worn I Heart Illinois T-shirt.

Okay, she replied.

I've got an idea.

Lydia did, too, but was pretty sure hers wasn't the same.

Are you free tomorrow?

I work from ten to five.

Lydia thought, *But I could call in sick, then we could elope, if that's what you're thinking. You're not? That's okay.*

Marco texted, *How 'bout breakfast?*

I could do that. What time?

Eight?

Eight's good for me.

Good. I'll meet you at the diner at eight a.m.

Sounds good.

She waited, but he didn't text anything else, which was fine—more than fine. They had a breakfast date, sort of. She thought about going with messed-up hair and no makeup, like they'd been together all night and were taking a break because they were hungry and madly in love. That would really boost her street cred. But then Marco would see her with messed-up hair and no makeup, which would pretty much kill their relationship. No, she would meet him as her usual self. *Why are we even meeting?* She fell asleep pondering possibilities.

LYDIA WOKE up with her cheek pressed to a granny square. *That'll look pretty.* She winced. She had drooled on the square. *Nice.* She wiped it on Belle's dress on her bedspread and dragged herself out of bed. Some people sprang out of bed in the morning. She didn't understand how they did it. Maybe when she became an adult, she would get springy. Technically, legally, she supposed she was an adult, but she didn't feel like one. She'd never even had a boyfriend, a fact she would never admit. Actually, she had taken great pains to hide it. Oh, she'd had some near misses. They weren't all that near, but they were definite misses.

At some point in her freshman year, she'd faced facts. She just wasn't the kind of girl guys would be interested in. Her mother told her she would come into her own like a beautiful swan. Maybe her mother had forgotten where the swan came from—an ugly duckling. *Thanks, Mom.* That was about the same time Lydia stopped confiding in her mother and took control. It would be her decision. Lydia didn't want a boyfriend. She felt empowered. She was resolved.

Though she could have changed. She was also open-minded and flexible. As soon as someone put her resolve to the test, she would reconsider. But no one had ever put her resolve to the test. So Lydia had gone through high school alone but with lots of friends. She just didn't have boyfriends.

MARCO WAS EARLY. He sat in a booth near the back and drank coffee. It gave him time to consider how best to pitch his plan to Lydia. It was not without risk. In fact, it was downright ballsy. But the situation called for something bold.

He would have to get to the point fairly quickly, just in case she thought he'd invited her there for the wrong reason. He didn't want her to think he was interested in her. Sometimes girls got carried away. He'd learned that the hard way. So he would make it clear from the outset—he was in it for Theo. Theo cared for Allie, and Allie's business was in trouble. So helping Allie helped Theo. Lydia worked for Allie, so she would want to help Allie too.

The whole scheme had come to him when he'd learned Decker was also threatening Caroline's business. Lydia's mother worked for Caroline. If Caroline's business went under, her mother would lose her job. When Lydia said that might force them to move, it bothered him on principle. It was unfair, and no one should have to go through that—not Eve, not Caroline, not Allie, and especially not Lydia, because she was nice. He'd seen her at school, usually with her nose in a book or getting some award. She was smart. People liked her. He liked her. She didn't deserve to have her life turned upside down. Marco knew what that was like, so he wanted to help.

If everything worked out, maybe they'd grow to be friends. He liked talking with her. She was different, and she knew it. He usually dated popular girls. They were easy to be with. Neither was in it for deep conversation. They both knew what they wanted— each other. So it was always a win-win situation. Everything was up-front with no misunderstandings. Once he thought about it, he realized he had ever seen Lydia with a boyfriend—or girlfriend, for that matter. Maybe she wasn't the dating type, whatever that was. Not that he wanted to date her. *Where did that come from?* He wasn't interested in her like that. He was curious about her, and she made him think. Sometimes he wondered what she would think about something or what she might say, which was not what he did. Marco was not a guy who cared what people thought. She was messing with his head.

Lydia walked in and spotted him at once. She was wearing those red glasses of hers. *What would she look like without them? But then she wouldn't be Lydia.* She sat down across from him.

Once they'd ordered, he got straight to it. "I want to help Allie."

"Me, too, but how?"

She looked intensely curious, with a single strand of

reddish hair dangling over her eyebrow, nearly touching her eyelashes. It bugged him so much that he wanted to brush it out of the way. But that would have been weird. He had no business touching her face, which she would have no problem telling him. The thought amused him.

"What?"

"What do you mean, 'what'?"

"You were practically smiling."

He leaned back. "No, I wasn't."

He could see in her eyes that she didn't believe him, but she didn't push it, because she was nice.

Moving on quickly, Marco said, "I've been thinking about how we could help her."

"We? I'm already helping her. I work for her. I'm there for support. How can you help her?"

Marco leaned forward and lowered his voice when he said, "Well, I have an idea."

"Ideas are good."

He said slowly, "Yeah." *Man, she's weird. And that hair is still there.* He couldn't stand it. "Excuse me. Sorry, but—" He reached over and brushed it back off her forehead. He did it quickly. There was no need to make a big production out of it. *It's just hair.* "How was that not driving you nuts? It was bothering me."

"Sorry."

She looked confused, but he was more confused.

Lydia's voice sounded just a bit breathy when she said, "So, what's your idea?"

"Right. My idea."

Nearly two hours later, Lydia said, "It got quiet." She looked around, and the diner had cleared out from the breakfast rush. They'd spent the time, heads together, in intense conversation. She glanced at her watch and inhaled sharply. "Oh my gosh, it's almost ten! I've got to go!"

"Okay, Cinderella."

She fished money out of her purse. "What? Oh. Ha. Funny."

"Never mind. Go. See you tomorrow night, six thirty sharp."

"I'll be there. See you then."

"I'M REALLY SORRY. Thanks for understanding." Allie hung up the phone. She'd just had to cancel an order from one of her favorite vendors. She stared at the spreadsheet on her monitor. *How else can I cut corners?* She scanned it twice then buried her face in her hands.

A knock on the door startled her. She looked up to find Eve waving. Allie went to the door.

"Hey, it's my late day, so I brought us all coffee on my way to work. Is this a bad time?"

Allie tried to look as though everything was fine, not that Eve would buy that. "No. Come on in."

Eve walked to the shop doorway and looked in. "Where's Lydia?"

"She's not here yet."

Eve shook her head adamantly. "She left the house early this morning." She looked at her watch. "Isn't she due here by now?"

Lydia rushed in and threw her bag down beside the coatrack. "I'm sorry! I lost track of the time! I'll make it up over lunch or at the end of the day—whatever you want. Or better yet, dock me."

"I'm not going to dock you." It didn't feel right to tell Eve, but Allie had ducked into the diner for a bagel to go, and she saw her with Marco. She couldn't blame her. Those Silva boys were something.

"Oh, she'll work it off," Eve assured her.

Lydia rushed to the shop entrance and unlocked it.

Eve said, "So, now that Lydia's accounted for, what's up with you? You looked pretty intense when I got here."

"Money." She tried to sound cheery. "But things will pick up. I'll be fine." She was lying. The shop would not be fine. It might take a few months and the small sum her grandparents had left her, but Decker was winning. The store was hers outright, but bills had to be paid. Property taxes would be due soon, and she would have to make payroll or let Lydia go. That would ruin Lydia's plan to work and go to college. Then there were the matters of food and her car payment. She could live without cable, but she wasn't sure what more she could cut. With a nod, she repeated, "I'll be fine."

Eve had that look she got when she was thinking intently, but her mood suddenly lightened. "How's Theo?"

Allie smiled. "I'm sure Theo is fine."

"Let me rephrase that. How are you and Theo—as a couple?"

Allie's eyes shone as she said in a whisper, "I think we actually are a couple, but I'm afraid to say it out loud. I don't want to jinx it."

Eve looked genuinely happy.

"He's so nice!" Allie leaned closer. "Really nice."

Eve's face lit up almost as much as Allie's. "I know!"

"He wanted me to know he would be there for me —through all this stuff that's going on. No matter where our relationship went, he would be there. Even if it's just as a friend."

Eve frowned.

Allie lifted an eyebrow. "He sure didn't kiss like a friend."

Eve laughed. "Allie, you're blushing!"

Allie put her hand to her cheek and confessed, "I'm crazy about him."

The bell rang lightly as the shop door opened. For a fleeting moment, Allie thought it might be a customer, but she heard Caroline's voice. She greeted Lydia then popped her head in the doorway.

Eve looked at her watch and told Caroline, "I'm on my way."

"No, you're fine. I just stopped by to make sure we're all on for tonight."

Eve nodded confidently. "I wouldn't miss it for anything. When Decker presents his plans, he'll have our lovely faces staring him down."

Allie nodded but felt as if she might lose her breakfast.

Apparently picking up Allie's true feelings, Caroline shook a fist in the air. "We are strong! We will be triumphant!"

Allie shook her fist too. "Absolutely!" *Maybe!*

She envied Caroline's indomitable spirit. Caroline would be fine, no matter what happened. Knowing Caroline and how successful she was, she'd stashed a nice sum of cash away over the years. That had to help. Not having to worry about housing and food tended to bolster one's spirits.

EIGHTEEN

ALLIE WAS ready ten minutes early. *Good for you. You can do this.*

She was nervous about attending the planning board meeting. It would be painful enough to see Decker forever change the face of Pine Harbor from the small town she loved to a tourist attraction. But as he unfolded his plan, he would destroy Pine Harbor's unspoiled coastline, quiet way of life, and small businesses—her small business. Her shop was not just a business. It contained family memories. Her grandparents had left it to her, trusting that she would keep their legacy going.

Pine Harbor relied on tourism in the summer but on a scale that had never altered the quaint working fishing village it had always been. That was why people loved to visit. Pine Harbor was just the right size with just the right balance of historic charm and modern convenience to draw visitors who shared its vision. It had no bold signs or expansive parking lots. There was simply the harbor, its boats, a few yachts, and locally owned seafood shacks and small shops. In short, it was the perfect retreat by the sea, and she loved it. And Decker was going to ruin it all —and her.

The thing about people with power was they usually won. At least, that had been Allie's experience. She had seen it in the workings of her small town, and she'd seen it on a national scale. People didn't play fairly. They manipulated their way through life and usually came out on top. She had no illusions about what would happen that evening. She and her friend would put up a fight. They would make their voices heard. She would be proud to stand beside people with integrity. But the world was run by money and power, and she had neither. The story of David and Goliath was a great one, but in real life, Goliath almost always won.

When Theo called and offered to drive her, she'd resisted at first. Allie was strong and independent and didn't need anyone to lean on. She'd been on her own for years, running her shop and her life. Even when she was with Justin, they were always two separate people with separate lives that intersected when convenient, like a romantic Venn diagram instead of a heart. She didn't want to fall into the same pattern with Theo.

Theo was different, and she was different with him. He never made her feel as though he was trying to take over her life. He was just there for her. They had a connection, unseen but deeply felt. It was a powerful force that she could not ignore. So she took Theo up on his offer to come with her to the meeting, and she was glad that she had.

Allie took one last look in the mirror. She looked neat, professional, and poised—not at all like she felt, which was good.

A knock sounded at the back door below. It had to be Theo, precisely on time. Suddenly, Allie remembered her phone. *And my watch. Oh, and I forgot to put on my earrings.* She scurried over to her dresser. They were where she'd left them. She wasn't ready. She didn't want to be ready. After shoving her phone and earrings into her purse, she slid her watch onto her wrist then went down the stairs. Panting, she opened the door.

Theo's eyes softened. "Are you okay?"

"Yes, absolutely. No, I'm not." There was no use trying to hide it from him.

He was so unbelievably calm. "It's okay. We've got time. Let's take a minute."

She took a step backward so he could come inside.

Theo drew her into his arms and gently pushed the door closed with his foot. "You'll be fine—better than fine."

She made a face and exhaled. "You seem awfully sure of yourself—or of me."

A smile lit his eyes. "I am. You can handle this."

That instilled her with confidence. "Yes, I can." She slowly nodded, as if each bob of her head would make it so.

Theo slid his hands down her arms and led her by the hand to the window facing the harbor. "Look out there. What do you see?"

"Pine Harbor, my home. This is where I was born and grew up. The people who came before me lived and worked here. My roots are here." She pointed at her hair. "And here."

They both burst out laughing, then tears came to her eyes. Sudden anger roiled within her. *Dammit.* She had never liked roller coasters, especially emotional ones.

"I see this shop and everything my grandparents put into it. They trusted me, but it's all slipping away."

Theo said, "I see what you see. You're standing on a foundation that was built over a century ago. Use that history. Your family and their love are your strength. So tap into that and fight for what's yours."

Allie drew in a big breath and blew it out. "Okay. Okay, I'm ready."

"That's my girl. Let's go kick Decker's ass!"

And together, they rode into battle.

LYDIA ARRIVED at the planning board meeting with her mother and spied Marco in a back corner, focused on his laptop. Caroline came over to Eve, which gave Lydia the perfect opportunity to slip away and join Marco. She sat down beside him. "Did you get it?"

He nodded. "I parked outside his office and waited for two hours. I was beginning to wonder if he'd taken the day off to prepare for the meeting at home. I don't even want to think about what we would have done then."

"Probably nothing?"

"Exactly."

"And he didn't see you?"

"No.

"So you've got it." He had already told her he had. She just couldn't believe he had done it.

"It was surprisingly easy. I got through the firewall, and there was no VPN." He shrugged and looked into Lydia's eyes, and he started to laugh. "Those pics you sent were amazing!"

She grinned proudly. "I know!"

He grew serious. "Okay, so here's what I need you to do. Decker's computer is hardwired to the display. The guy's such a Luddite. He's made this so easy. I could probably override it through the Wi-Fi, but it would be even easier if you just unplugged the cable."

Lydia panicked. "Me?"

"Yes. Everyone knows you and trusts you. They would never suspect you if you wandered by and just casually kicked the cord loose. While you do that, I need to stay here and mess with the Bluetooth. Look, see the blue cord up there? That's the one." When Lydia hesitated, he looked at her urgently. "Do it now."

Despite her sheer dread, Lydia nodded and left.

ALLIE AND THEO walked into the meeting room. Theo gave Allie's hand a squeeze, then they joined Eve and Caroline.

They were all on their way to sit down when Theo said, "Be right back," and disappeared in the direction of the restrooms. Allie glanced about then quickly regretted it.

"Allie."

"Justin." She hadn't spoken with him since their meeting on the dock a week earlier. While they had parted on good terms, Allie still wasn't ready to casually run into him by chance. He, on the other hand, seemed to have recovered quite nicely. In fact, he looked delighted as he approached—with his date. *Who brings a date to a planning board meeting?*

"Allie, you know Jocelyn, don't you? From high school?"

Bossy Jossy? "Yes, of course I remember. Good to see you again."

They all held their smiles just a moment too long.

Allie broke the silence. "Come here often?"

Justin had an expression she couldn't quite read.

His date answered, "We're just here for Decker's presentation. I'm Decker's administrative assistant, so he asked me to be here just in case. But as soon as he's finished, Justin and I are going out to celebrate."

"Oh." *Celebrate?* She knew she should ask and wasn't sure what was holding her back.

Maybe it was the uncomfortable look on her ex-boyfriend's face. He said, "I was going to stop by and tell you, but since we're all here..."

Jocelyn blurted, "We're engaged."

Allie's eyes opened so wide that she thought they might roll out of their sockets, but she recovered. "*Engaged?*" *Wow, that was quick. Guess I didn't break your heart after all. Yay. Happy ending.*

Justin said, "As of this morning."

Was there a shotgun involved?

In a gesture Allie felt certain that Jocelyn been doing all day to anyone who stood still long enough, Jocelyn extended her left hand to show off her ring. *Her* ring. It was *Allie's* ring. Although technically, it wasn't, since it had never been in her possession. But that was the ring. She would never forget it. While Jocelyn wiggled her fingers, Allie's fingers were busy counting the days. That same ring had been offered to her eight days earlier. Allie was too shell-shocked to care how she looked anymore, but she noticed the happy couple was staring at her. It was her turn to say something.

"What a beautiful ring. And what a surprise." She made eye contact with Justin. *Good. Squirm.*

"I know! We'd been dating on and off for a while, but when you turned him down—oops, sorry." Jocelyn wrinkled her face as her eyes darted from Justin to Allie as if she were in the front row at Wimbledon. "I didn't mean—but well, anyway, he surprised me!"

Wait a minute. You'd been dating on and off? For a while? Allie wondered. *How long is a while?* It was probably more than eight days, which would put their courtship concurrent with hers and Justin's—which had not been on and off. She met Justin's guilty gaze then suddenly wanted to laugh in the way that bubbled up in the middle of church or at a funeral—or a funeral in a church. She faked a coughing fit to cover it up then thanked God that Theo reappeared at her side to deflect the attention.

Theo reached out and shook Justin's hand, then Allie took matters into her own hands.

"This is Justin's fiancée."

Jocelyn held out her left hand to Theo. While Allie plotted their escape, Theo graciously said all the right things. Then he deftly made an excuse and whisked Allie away. *How did he do that? Doesn't matter. It's done. He's my hero.*

The meeting was called to order. They had no time to talk except for Theo to lean over and whisper, "I hope they'll be very happy." Only a spark in his eyes betrayed any hint of amusement.

On Allie's other side, Eve gestured toward Marco and Lydia and murmured, "What's up with those two?"

They were in the back row with their heads together.

Allie looked over and shrugged. She turned to Theo and whispered, "Are Marco and Lydia... together?"

He shook his head. Allie turned to Eve and shook her head as well. Then the meeting began.

NINETEEN

DECKER STEPPED to the podium and opened his laptop. Directly behind him, the monitor displayed a lovely rendering of the new Pine Harbor as he declared, "Welcome to Wilmington Dunes, a state-of-the-art development that will breathe new life into our community and bring hundreds of jobs."

Caroline muttered to Eve, "I liked our old life."

Eve added, "And our old jobs."

Decker smiled at the crowd with a confident air. "A gentle slope from the imported white sand beach is a multitiered condo community, where guests can work out in a state-of-the-art gym or enjoy a leisurely stroll along our synthetic boardwalk."

He clicked for the next slide. On the screen behind him was a photo of a man walking across a bed of nails.

Despite a low murmur, Decker continued. "Or

guests may follow a private footpath to the sea, where their own private beach awaits them for a leisurely afternoon in the sun." *Click*. The slide showed a patch of wet sand with a beach towel spread out. Painted on it was a police chalk outline of a dead body.

Apparently absorbed in his notes, Decker seemed unaware of the crowd's uneasy snickers. He said, "On the ground floor of the condos, guests will delight in the stylish restaurants and shops at their disposal." *Click*. A disheveled woman clad in a housecoat and hair rollers with a cigarette hanging tenuously from her lips, seemingly held on by day-old red lipstick, stood in a grocery aisle, holding a box of dry cat food.

Decker pressed on. "The kids will love this amphibious ride." *Click*. On the screen, an alligator was poised to emerge from the edge of a swamp.

The laughs and murmurs grew louder.

LOOKING CONFUSED, Decker turned toward the screen, but Marco and Lydia had worked out a system. She was keenly focused on Decker, and he stared at his laptop. Lydia nudged Marco any time Decker made a slight move. Their slides alternated with Decker's so that they could switch in an instant to ensure Decker only saw the slides he expected to see.

Looking puzzled, Decker turned back to his laptop and continued, "Beside the condos, a five-star waterfront inn will await road-weary guests." *Click.* An iconic neon sign read Bates Motel: Vacancy.

Jocelyn walked along the wall toward the podium and waved to get Decker's attention, but he was too absorbed in the slideshow and the audience's reaction to notice her.

Decker cleared his throat. "I don't know about you, but my mouth is watering over this soon-to-be Michelin-starred farm-to-table cuisine served on our open-air rooftop deck." *Click.* In the parched desert landscape, buzzards feasted on a half-decomposed steer.

By that point, Marco had gotten into a rhythm—old slide, wait a beat, then new slide. Then Decker would turn, and the sequence would repeat. The robust laughter destroyed any composure Decker had left.

Jocelyn stepped toward the stage, cupped her hands around her mouth, and whispered loudly, "Decker!"

He glanced at her and tried to shoo her away. When she whispered again, he said through clenched teeth, "Not now!"

Beads of sweat dotted his forehead as he soldiered on. "Pine Harbor will become a highly sought-out convention and wedding venue with our stunning

Wilmington Ballroom." *Click*. Children with birthday-cake-encrusted cheeks frolicked in a ball pit.

Decker whipped his head around, but Marco was too fast for him. On the home stretch, Decker arrived at his grand finale, which was supposed to have string quartet music accompanying a beautiful couple walking down a path that wended its way through swaying seagrass-topped dunes. Decker delivered the final line of his pitch. "Wilmington Dunes: embrace the romance." *Click*.

Decker turned. On the screen, seated in formal attire, a nose flute quartet played. Marco left the slide on for Decker to see while laughter erupted.

At first, Decker's mouth hung agape, then he sputtered out an attempt to explain. "That's not—I don't know what this is, but—" If he finished, no one heard him. He slammed down the lid of his laptop and stormed out.

Marco fist-bumped Lydia, and they beamed triumphantly.

That was until they heard a familiar voice. "Marco." Behind them, arms folded, stood Theo.

Twenty minutes later, the planning board had adjourned to a conference room, where Marco and

Lydia stood at one end of a large conference table, Decker sat at the other, and the planning board sat in between.

Decker lifted his chin and glared. "I demand an apology."

Lydia took in a breath, but Marco nudged her as he reached into his pocket. A folded paper fell to the table. "Oops." He held it up casually. "What's this?" Marco made a show of reading closely. "Oh, it's just a copy of a receipt from an exterminator, Dead Bug Walking." He looked straight at Decker, held his gaze for several seconds, then folded it up and put it back into his pocket. "I'm sorry, what were you saying?" He tilted his head and practically dared Decker to repeat his demand.

Decker looked as though steam might come out of his ears, but he calmed himself and said sheepishly, "I'm willing to accept an apology, and we can let the whole thing go."

One of the planning board members, a real estate attorney, said, "You'd be within your rights to take them to court."

Lydia trembled, unsure of whether she would faint or throw up. Decker shook his head with pompous magnanimity. "I don't think that will be necessary. As they say, boys will be boys." For the first time, he seemed to notice Lydia, so he added, "And girls." His eyebrows drew together, and he opened his mouth and thought for a moment. "Never mind."

The chair of the planning board looked at Marco and Lydia. "Do you two have anything to say?"

Lydia said softly, "We're sorry."

Not quite as contritely, Marco muttered, "Yeah, sorry."

Satisfied, the chair turned to Decker. "We'd be happy to view your actual presentation at this time." She then turned to Marco and Lydia. "You two may go."

THE NEXT MORNING, Lydia and Marco cleaned the Silva Brothers men's room. When they were done, they packed up their supplies and emerged in the doorway on their way to the ladies' room.

Theo called from a table by the window, where Eve and Allie sat with him, having breakfast. "I'll be in to check your work in a minute."

Marco and Lydia made eye contact but moved on to the next item on what Theo and Eve had called their community service list.

Eve asked, "Do you think we were too harsh?"

Theo said, "No."

Allie looked at him with eyes full of sympathy.

"But they were just trying to help." Before Theo could respond, Allie's phone signaled an incoming text. "It's from Caroline. She says, 'Major breakthrough! Kim and I have tapped into the rumor mill. A copy of the receipt from Dead Bug Walking has made the rounds via text, and a doctor friend debunked the Gallery infection. We're in business again!'"

While Allie was reading, a text came in from Kim. "Celebrating! See you soon!" she read.

Theo headed for the bar. "This calls for champagne!"

A loud knock came from the bar entrance. Allie got up, but Theo said, "No, I'll get it." He lifted the champagne. "If it's an intruder, I've got a weapon." He unlocked the door.

"Let me help you with that." Kim walked in, followed closely by Caroline, and took the bottle from Theo. As they passed by the bathrooms, Theo called, "Come here, you two!"

When Marco and Lydia emerged, Theo said, "Marco, make the two of you a couple of Shirley Temples and come over here."

Kim popped the cork. "And bring some glasses!"

Theo conferred with Eve, then said, "Your community service sentences have been commuted."

Marco and Lydia hastened to put away their cleaning supplies and join the others.

Kim offered a toast. "Here's to Pine Harbor and small businesses everywhere! May Decker Wilmington never come near them again!"

The celebration had arrived at a slight lull when Caroline got a text. She looked up. "Ladies and gentlemen, I have news." A sudden silence descended. "It hasn't been made public, but I have some contacts, and... the planning board has turned down Decker's application."

A cheer erupted. Kim sprang to her feet and began dancing while the others toasted and hugged one another. Except Marco and Lydia, who exchanged satisfied grins and fist-bumped each other.

TWENTY

*W*EEKS *later*

Theo carried a picnic basket with one hand and held Allie's hand with the other as they walked to their favorite spot on his future parcel of land. He set down the basket and turned to her. "Do you know what this is?"

"A hill overlooking the harbor?"

Theo blinked slowly. "Let me rephrase that. Do you know what *day* this is?"

"Saturday?" She had no idea what he was getting at.

He shook his head, but his mouth curved up at the corner. "Allie Pidgeon. It's our anniversary!"

She narrowed her eyes but didn't bother with the math. "We haven't known each other long enough for an anniversary."

"A month. It's our one-month anniversary. You're not exactly the romantic type, are you?"

"Yes! I am, but I was lost for a minute." She smiled warmly. "Happy anniversary."

He kissed her, and she was quickly on board with the concept.

He took her hands in his. "You know, sometimes couples like to celebrate their anniversaries by returning to where they first met." His eyes lit up as his mouth spread into a broad smile.

Allie winced. "You're not going to let me forget that, are you?"

"No. But I decided to celebrate here instead."

"Good call."

Theo's smile faded. "It's only been a month, but I thought I should give you a heads-up."

"A heads-up?"

"Or a head start—in case you want to run."

"Theo, what are you talking about?"

"I don't want to scare you, but at some point in the future—the way-distant future—I might fall in love."

Allie smiled. "Thanks for the warning."

"So you're okay with that?"

"Do I look like I'm running?" Joy welled up inside her, and she grinned. She couldn't help it.

He smiled, looking relieved. "No, but you're quick."

"I'm not going anywhere."

"Good." Theo took Allie's face in his hands and kissed her.

COMING NEXT

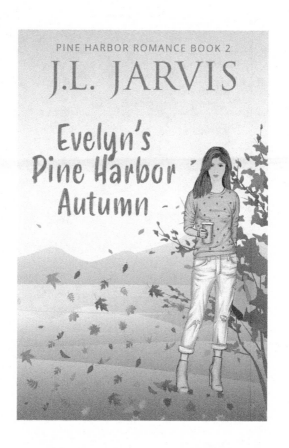

PINE HARBOR ROMANCE BOOK 2

J.L. JARVIS

Evelyn's
Pine Harbor
Autumn

THANK YOU!

Thank you, reader. With so many options, I appreciate your choosing my book to read. Your opinion matters, so please consider sharing a review to help other readers.

ALSO BY J.L. JARVIS

For more books by J.L. Jarvis, visit:

jljarvis.com

Or find them at your favorite bookstore:

Amazon ❧ Angus & Robertsons ❧ Apple ❧ Audible ❧
Barnes & Noble ❧ Book Depository ❧ Books-a-Million ❧
Books2Read ❧ Booktopia ❧ Google ❧ Hudson Booksellers
❧ Indigo ❧ Kobo ❧ Powell's ❧ Schuler Books ❧ Walmart
❧ Waterstones

BOOK NEWS

Would you like to know when the next book comes
out? Sign up for book release news at:
news.jljarvis.com

ACKNOWLEDGMENTS

Editing by Red Adept Editing
redadeptediting.com

ABOUT THE AUTHOR

J.L. Jarvis is a left-handed opera singer/teacher/lawyer who writes books. She received her undergraduate training from the University of Illinois at Urbana-Champaign and a doctorate from the University of Houston. She now lives and writes in New York.

Sign up to be notified of book releases and related news:
news.jljarvis.com

Contact JL here:
jljarvis.com/contact
-or-
Email her at:
author@jljarvis.com

Follow JL online at:
jljarvis.com

facebook.com/jljarvis1writer

twitter.com/JLJarvis_writer

bookbub.com/authors/j-l-jarvis

pinterest.com/jljarviswriter

Made in the USA
Coppell, TX
06 July 2020